CHRISTMAS CORPSE

A CHRISTMAS COZY MYSTERY SERIES

MONA MARPLE

CHRISTMAS COZY MYSTERY BONUSES

Help yourself to a festive fun pack, available exclusively at:

https://dl.bookfunnel.com/9ckxf7kcfh

Ho-ho-hope you enjoy it!

Mona x

1

I groaned as the festive chatter of the radio DJ ended, and the next song began. *Driving Home For Christmas*. Of course. I rolled my eyes and turned the dial, but of course the old rust bucket of a car couldn't find any other stations for me to listen to.

I turned the volume down, then felt an enormous yawn build inside me, and turned it back up again.

The merry cheer might not be the company I wanted, but it was the best that was available. And even in my forlorn state, I could see the irony of having to listen to that particular song as I did, indeed, drive home for Christmas.

If only my home wasn't empty, maybe I'd be able to share the good feelings. I'd been a lover of all things Christmas once upon a time. But where was the sense in trimming up the house and making Christmas dinner, just for me? The empty house waiting for me was why I'd worked so late, I knew, even as I told my co-workers that I just wanted to leave things all neat for the next person.

It was the last working day before Christmas and the rest of the clinic staff had darted out of the place at 5pm exactly, most of them wearing a Christmas jumper or a pair of festive earrings. Some even had a strand of tinsel wrapped around their ponytails.

I'd been living the high life as a locum GP for the last nine months, but the woman whose maternity leave I had been covering would return to her old post in the New Year, meaning I was out of a job and out of excuses not to spend more time in my empty house.

I rolled the window down a little and shivered as the frigid air joined me inside the vehicle. Setting off home without a warmer change of clothes wasn't my best idea. My silk blouse, pencil skirt and heels were basic office attire but the car's heater had given up months ago. The yawns were worrying me, though, and I knew a blast of cold air was a good way to help me stay alert.

The snow was coming thick and fast and I'd lost my sense of direction. I hadn't passed the exit, I was sure of that. The problem was that everything looked the same covered in the white blanket that the snow provided.

I jumped at the sound of my phone ringing. My ancient Bluetooth system somehow connected the phone to the car, but the screen didn't reveal who the caller was. It made every call an adventure.

"Hello? Can you hear me?" I asked. I didn't trust the Bluetooth completely.

"Holly!"

"August?" I asked. My sister was, you guessed it, an August baby. I was a Christmas baby and just grateful my parents named me Holly instead of December.

"Hey! Merry Christmas!"

"Merry Christmas!" I replied. My sister's enthusiasm was infectious, that was for sure.

"Are you driving? In the storm?"

"I'm being safe, don't worry. Anyway, I'm the big sister, I'm the one who should worry."

"Oh, sure, you can worry about me. My life is super exciting and risky right now!"

"How is Jeb?"

"Adorable! But I'm not having this conversation while you're driving."

"I'm fine!" I insisted.

"Nope, no way. What would mu…"

"Okay, fine, I'll let you go," I interrupted.

"Holly…" my sister said. She knew exactly what I was doing. I heard Jeb begin to fuss in the background.

"You go, we'll speak soon. I love you," I said.

"I love you too," August replied.

I ended the call and pictured the way her brow would furrow with concern for a moment, until her hunky husband Tom handed baby Jeb to her and she returned to her perfect life. I didn't begrudge her having all she had. Trust me, if anyone deserved perfect, it was August. It just made it harder to ignore how much of a failure I was when I had her as my little sister. Not even my big sister! I was supposed to be the one who took the lead and set the example.

I smiled and shook my head. August was my best friend. And she'd taken it well when I'd turned down the invitation to join her for Christmas. I usually spent the holiday with her, in her cute little cottage that looked fresh out of Good Housekeeping, but I didn't want to intrude this year. Not baby Jeb's first Christmas. That should be an occasion that August and Tom got to themselves.

I'd be fine. Christmas would be different, of course, but the fact was it had been different ever since our mum had died. The magic of the season seemed to have left us, or me at least, when she did.

The radio DJ read out a warning about heavy snow and I wondered if I'd be able to make it to the supermarket before the place closed. I'd put it off right to the last minute. If I couldn't get there, it really would be a pitiful Christmas Day. I'd probably end up eating ramen from the cupboard.

I laughed at the thought of that, but the grin was wiped off my face as I felt the car lose control. I recognised the sensation of planing across ice, but how could that be possible? The snow was so deep. Was there black ice hidden under the fresh snowfall?

I remembered to steer into the skid, even as every part of my body wanted to fight against it. It was no use, the car was going to end up wherever the ice took it, and I felt grateful that nobody else was crazy enough to be out on the road. At least there was no chance of me hitting another car.

That thought made me smile, and then the car collided with something, and there was a wallop against the windscreen as a fresh load of snow was dislodged. I shivered. I couldn't feel my toes anymore.

I suddenly felt incredibly tired. It had been such a busy week, and really I had nothing to rush home for.

I decided to close my eyes, just for a moment.

2

In the dream, I was warm. So warm that I wanted to tell someone to turn the heat down a little. Except nobody was there. It was just me, surrounded by a dazzling white light, getting hotter and hotter.

The rap-rap-rap made my eyes flutter open, but I was still surrounded by dazzling white, so I closed them again. It was too bright, and too hot.

I felt hands on me then, heard a gasp, felt someone attempt to shake me.

"Oh, finally, can you turn the heat down?" I asked. "Please?"

"Goodness," came the reply, and something about the voice made me snap my eyes open. Right there, her face in my face, was a small woman with silver hair, bright eyes and the most elaborate red dress I'd ever seen in my life.

I gazed at her and wondered if I was dreaming.

"You're frozen, dear. We have to get you out of here. Can you move?"

"No, no, I'm hot. Not cold."

The woman frowned at me. "It's worse than I imagined then. We have to move quickly. What's your name, dear?"

"Holly," I said. "Holly Wood."

"Well, that's a good sign. If you're well enough to joke..."

"I'm not joking. That's really my name," I insisted. She wasn't the first person to think it was a joke.

"Okay then, Holly, I'm Mrs Claus, and that's not a joke either. I'm going to count to three and then I'm pulling you out. If you can help, please do."

The woman – surely she wasn't really called Mrs Claus – counted down and then pulled me out of the vehicle with a strength that came as a surprise.

Outside, the sky had grown dark and the snow was still falling. I surveyed the scene. The front of my car had slammed right into a mound of snow, the windscreen was covered, and the fresh snowfall was halfway up the tyres.

"How did you see me?" I asked.

"Thankfully, you'd left your lights on. I was driving by and saw them. I'm so glad I found you, dear. How long were you stuck there?"

"Only a second, I just closed my eyes for a... what time is it?"

"It's the middle of the night! Almost 8pm!"

"That can't be possible. I left work at six, so I must have crashed at half past at the latest. Have I really been there that long?"

The woman pretending to be Mrs Claus shuddered at the thought and led me towards the only other car in sight.

"Whoa! This is yours?"

The woman beamed with pride. "It certainly is. It's a 1959 Cadillac. I call her Baby."

"She's beautiful. Are you sure it's no trouble to take me... where are you taking me?"

"I'll take you home to Candy Cane Hollow, dear. We'll get the doctor to check you over. Now, come on in."

"Candy Cane Hollow? I've never heard of a place by that name."

"We're kind of off the beaten track," the woman said with a wink.

"And you're really telling me your name is Mrs Claus?"

"I am indeed. And a lady named Holly Wood surely understands what a predicament a name can be," she said with a chuckle as she turned the key and the engine roared to life.

I watched as we passed my car. I'd have to organise a recovery truck to collect it. I felt bad that I'd be interrupting someone's Christmas break.

"Everyone teased me at school about my name. They asked what films I'd been in. Even the careers advisor assumed I wanted to be an actor!"

"Oh, that's a shame. There are sweets in there, help yourself."

I opened the glove compartment and saw a stash of candy canes and a few chocolate Santas. I unwrapped the foil from a Santa and took a bite, let the sweet treat dissolve on my mouth.

"The sugar will help," Mrs Claus said.

"Are you a nurse?" I asked.

"No, no. I'm a mother, though. I've learned all kinds of tricks to help with injuries and illness."

"I don't have children," I admitted.

"You don't even look old enough!"

"That's very sweet, but I'm 29."

"You're a baby! There's time. Do you want children?"

"Yes," I admitted. "My sister's 23 years old, already

married with a baby, lives in this beautiful cottage, has her life all sorted."

"And you want that too?"

"Doesn't everyone?" I asked.

Mrs Claus frowned a little. "I think some people never really know what they want. I've always imagined that that must be a dreadful shame. So many possibilities out there, and to not know which you want. It sounds to me, dear Holly, that you know what you want and you have plenty of time to find it. I'd say that makes you very blessed."

I felt a shudder across my spine. I really was freezing. How could I have ever believed that I was too hot?

"I haven't really thought of it that way before. You're right. Thank you."

"You're most welcome! I know that I can interfere some-times, so please tell me if I overstep the mark. We'll soon be in Candy Cane Hollow. You'll love it!"

Despite my earlier funk, I found myself smiling at Mrs Claus and looking out the window with excitement. We took an exit I'd never seen before and within seconds passed a charming sign that welcomed us to Candy Cane Hollow.

I saw the lights up ahead and gasped as we drove past the largest Christmas tree I'd ever seen. It was decked out in baubles and lights that twinkled and surrounded by a group of people singing.

"That's the choir, dear. They're really very good."

After that, we reached the village itself and I had to rub my eyes to believe what I was seeing. It was so quaint, with old buildings and tasteful Christmas lights strewn across each street.

We drove slowly by a butchers, a bakers, and a book-shop. A few people milled around, most carrying bags, and each and every one stopped what they were doing and waved as we passed.

Mrs Claus gave me a brief explanation of who each person was, and seemed genuinely delighted to have seen all of them.

"Does everyone know each other here?" I asked.

"But of course!" Mrs Claus exclaimed.

"I don't even know the people who live next door to me," I admitted. I sent them a Christmas card every year in a bid to learn their names, and although they responded each year by popping a card through my letterbox, I could never read the handwriting to decipher their names.

"Have they just moved in? You could bake cookies for them as a housewarming treat. Nobody can say no to home baked treats."

I smiled at the easy way that Mrs Claus viewed the world. Unfortunately, the neighbours had been there before me, and I'd been there for five years, so I couldn't blame our stalled relationship on their new arrival.

"This place is beautiful," I said.

"It's really something, isn't it?"

"I can't believe I've never heard of it."

"Well, there are lots of small places that time seems to forget. You know where it is now, dear, and you're always welcome."

"Thank you," I said as we pulled up outside a small doctor's clinic. I got out of the car, feeling a twinge in my neck as I did, and entered after Mrs Claus.

A slender woman in a red turtleneck was partway through painting her nails when we entered. She glanced up and grinned.

"Mrs Claus! What a wonderful surprise! How are you? How's Nick?"

"Hello, Persephone, dear. Is Sirus around?"

"Of course!" The receptionist jumped up from the desk, teetered across the room on impossibly high heels, and knocked on a door marked *Dr Lancaster*. A booming voice told her to enter, and she disappeared into the room.

A moment later, she returned and ushered us into the doctor's room.

"Mrs Claus! What can I do for you?" Dr Lancaster asked as we all took seats inside. He was a big bear of a man and the pen he picked up from his desk looked tiny in his paw of a hand.

"It's not me, dear, it's Holly here. I found her inside her car out on the main road. There'd been a snow drift. We think she'd been inside the vehicle for more than an hour."

Dr Lancaster raised a bushy eyebrow and directed me to lie on the bed in the corner of the room. I did as he said.

He told me to close my eyes and tell him when I felt him touch me with what looked like a lollipop stick. I closed my eyes and waited.

"Hmm," Dr Lancaster said. I opened my eyes in alarm. Hmm was never the reaction I wanted from a doctor. I looked at my body and saw that he was pressing the lollipop stick into my arm. I couldn't feel it at all.

"That's not good, right?"

"Did you lose consciousness at all before Mrs Claus found you?"

I shifted on the bed. "I think I was unconscious pretty much all of that time."

Dr Lancaster gave a whistle. "You've got a fairly mild case of frostbite, Ms..."

"Wood. Holly Wood," I said.

"Really?" He raised an eyebrow again.

"Yes! Really!" I said with a laugh.

"Okay then. Mild frostbite. You need to gradually warm your body up. It has to be gradual, that's the key thing. You'll be fine, but you may want to say thank you to Mrs Claus."

"Oh, stop," Mrs Claus objected.

"She saved your life, Ms Wood," Dr Lancaster said, and I gulped as I realised how close I had come to dying.

3

Back in the waiting room, the receptionist eyed me suspiciously in between finishing off her bright red nails. A half-eaten mince pie sat by her side on the desk. Homemade, of course.

"You're not from here," she said.

"No," I said. "It's a wonderful place, though. I really like it."

"Well, don't get any ideas. We're full."

"You're full?" I repeated, with a laugh.

"Every house is taken and every job is filled. Mrs Claus has a habit of rescuing waifs and strays, but just remember that this isn't your home and you don't belong here."

"Wow," I said under my breath.

Mrs Claus burst out of the doctor's room then, complete with a paper bag that I guessed held whatever medicine Dr Lancaster had prescribed. She beamed at me, then turned to Persephone and gave an equally warm smile to her.

I wondered if what Persephone had said was true. Did Mrs Claus make a habit of bringing people home? I could believe it. She seemed the sort of person who wouldn't be able to stand the idea of someone having an aching heart or a hungry stomach.

"Ready, dear?" Mrs Claus asked.

"Yes," I said. "I'll ring for a breakdown service and be on my way home."

"Nonsense! You're coming home with me. I'll nurse you back to good health. Won't I, Persephone? Do you remember that year you had that dreadful sickness bug and I came over with my chicken soup? It was the only food you could face."

"I remember, Mrs Claus. Your chicken soup's the best! You and Nick really took good care of me."

I smiled at the thought. It sounded like Mr Claus was just as generous as his wife. I wondered if I'd get to meet him.

"Oh, Mrs Claus, we have the ice sculpting tomorrow, remember. You and Nick will still judge it, won't you?"

"Of course! Let me double check I have it written down. You know I'm only as good as my diary." Mrs Claus said. She reached into her handbag and pulled out a stunning leather planner, opened it to the next day's entry. Her handwriting was flawless.

"Ice sculpting?" I asked with a grin.

"I'm hoping to win," Persephone's eyes shone as she spoke.

"It's right here, dear. We're looking forward to it."

"Great! Well, tell Nick I said hi," Persephone said. She flashed Mrs Claus another winning smile, then returned her attention on finishing painting her nails.

"I want to say thank you," I said when we were back in the Cadillac. "You saved my life."

"Oh, nonsense. Dr Lancaster always has been dramatic!"

"No, he's right. I was out there literally freezing to death.

If you hadn't found me, I wouldn't have lasted until the morning," my voice shook as I spoke and a tear escaped me. I wiped it away but not fast enough.

"Oh, my dear Holly, come here. You're safe now, my love. You're safe," Mrs Claus pulled me to her and I allowed myself to sink into her embrace. It felt good to be comforted. Nobody had held me like that in years.

I pulled away and wiped my nose, and as I turned to reach for my seatbelt, I saw Persephone glaring at me from inside the doctor's surgery.

Claus Cottage sat right at the highest point of Candy Cane Hollow, overlooking the village itself. It was also not a cottage. Sure, it was presented in the style of a cottage, but it was enormous.

The light was on in every window and the outside façade was trimmed with twinkling fairy lights. A white cat sat in the window closest to the front door.

"Welcome to our home, Holly. Let's get you inside," Mrs Claus said with a smile. She looked as delighted as I felt to reach Claus Cottage.

I followed her down the path, our feet crunching through the snow. Again, I wished I'd planned ahead and taken some winter boots to work with me that morning. My heels did nothing to protect my feet. I wondered how Persephone managed. She'd probably been organised enough to pack sensible shoes for the trek home.

"We're home!" Mrs Claus called as she pushed the heavy oak door open. The cat came and fussed around her legs and she laughed like a schoolgirl. The house smelled like gingerbread and fir, and right there in the spacious hallway was a beautiful real Christmas tree, trimmed with red and green baubles.

"Your home is beautiful," I gushed.

"Oh, why thank you dear! That's so sweet of you to say. Claus Cottage has been in the family for generations, so I really can't take much credit. But I agree, it's a charming place. And this fussy little girl is Snowy."

I attempted to bend down to stroke the kitty, but the movement hurt more than I expected and I winced.

"Oh, where are my manners! Let's get you to the den," Mrs Claus said. She led me across the hallway and into a small, cosy room with a log fire burning. A large settee faced the fire and I collapsed onto it. Mrs Claus busied herself finding a pillow for my head and a blanket for my feet, then handed the TV remote to me.

"You've done so much for me," I said. I wanted to say more but I could feel my body growing weaker.

"Nonsense. Now, you relax, okay? I'm going to stay in here and work a while, so I'll be right here if you need anything. Shall I make you a nice mug of cocoa?"

The offer sounded divine, but my eyelids were growing heavy, and it took all the energy I had to shake my head.

I allowed my head to nestle into the pillow and drifted off to sleep.

When I awoke, the fire was burning just as bright and Mrs Claus was still in the room with me, although she had fallen asleep in a chair across the room.

"Mother!" A velvety voice came from the hallway, and Mrs Claus' eyes burst open.

"Shh! Shh!" She hissed and jumped up from her chair.

"What is it?"

"We have a visitor. She's asleep in there."

"A visitor? Now isn't the best time, mother!"

"Oh, nincompoop. She was stranded in a snow drift. Dr Lancaster diagnosed frost bite," Mrs Claus explained, her voice not quite as low as she probably imagined it to be.

I got up from the settee and approached the hallway, where I could see Mrs Claus in conversation with a man I presumed to be her son.

"Goodness. Is she okay?"

"She will be, but she needs to rest. Are you okay? You sounded panicked?"

"Mrs Claus?" I interrupted. I glanced from her to the

man, and then tried to close my jaw. Standing there in the hallway, in a pretty tight red t-shirt, was the most drool-worthy man I'd ever seen before in my life.

"Oh, Holly, this is my son. Nick, meet Holly Wood," Mrs Claus said with a twinkle in her eye.

"Holly Wood?" Nick asked with a smile that revealed a dimple in his cheek. I wondered if frost bite could make a person faint.

"Yes, Nick, you're not deaf. Now, Holly, how are you feeling, dear? You shouldn't be up!" Mrs Claus exclaimed.

"Oh, I'm fine. I'm good. I'll call for the breakdown service now and get out of your hair. I've imposed enough," I said. I tried to stare straight ahead, away from the wintry god who was looking at me with some amusement.

"You won't be going anywhere tonight. The snow hasn't stopped falling all night. The roads are closed," Nick said.

"But..." I began, then realised I had no idea how to finish the sentence. There was nobody waiting for me to return home, not even a cat to feed or a plant to water. Really, nobody would even notice whether I returned home. That was a sobering thought.

"You'll stay here, Holly. I've had a guest room prepared for you. Now, Nick, what's the matter?"

"Nothing now. I've had some missed calls from Dr Lancaster, but it must be him wanting to check on Holly."

It felt like I had been electrocuted hearing my name on his lips, but I tried not to react.

"Yes, probably. He's a very thorough doctor. I'll give him a call now."

Mrs Claus walked to a small, ornate table in the hallway and dialled a number.

"No answer. He must be busy."

Mrs Claus gently ushered me back into the den, and I was disappointed when I saw that Nick hadn't followed us.

"So, that's your son?" I said. It was the inanest thing I could have said, but maybe I could blame the frost bite.

"My Nick. That's him."

"Hold on, Nick Claus?"

Mrs Claus' eyes twinkled. "Shall we watch a Christmas movie, dear?"

"Sure," I agreed.

Mrs Claus sat next to me on the settee and spread the blanket across both of our laps. At first, I felt awkward sitting so close to someone I barely knew, but that feeling quickly passed.

As the film started, Nick appeared in the doorway with a mug in each hand.

"Cocoa?" He offered. He set one mug in front of me and the other in front of his mum. The hot drink smelled amazing and was topped with cream and grated nutmeg.

"This is incredible, thank you," I whispered.

To my absolute delight, Nick winked at me. Then the phone rang out in the hallway, and he left us to go and take the call.

I tried to listen to him more than the movie, because his voice was delicious and I wanted to soak it in as much as I could. No doubt the roads would be clear in the morning and I'd leave this winter wonderland and never see Nick, or Mrs Claus, again.

In fact, maybe I was still asleep in my car. Maybe this whole thing was a dream.

After a few murmured sounds, I very clearly heard Nick's voice rise. I felt Mrs Claus stiffen at the side of me. Apparently, she had been listening too. Well, she did say she liked to interfere.

We both waited, and Nick reappeared in the doorway after a few moments.

"Is everything okay, son?" Mrs Claus asked. Concern was etched across her face.

"No, mother, it isn't. That was Dr Lancaster on the phone. Persephone Hyde-Barker is dead. He believes she was poisoned!"

"This can't be true. We saw her earlier, Nick. She was alive and well earlier! She was her normal self!" Mrs Claus said.

I wondered if her normal self included the less than kind comments she'd said when Mrs Claus was out of earshot, but silently scolded myself for that thought.

"You saw her when you took Holly there to see Dr Lancaster?" Nick asked.

I nodded. "She's the receptionist, right? She was painting her fingernails and talking about the, erm, the ice..."

"The sculpting competition. Oh my! The judging was tomorrow! You know that Persephone loved that competition," Mrs Claus wailed.

"She did? I don't remember her entering before," Nick said.

"Hmm, you're right. Maybe a new interest for her. I know she was really looking forward to it. She made a point of reminding me about it today."

There was a knock at the door.

Nick cleared his throat and pulled open the heavy oak.

Two police officers stood on the other side of the door. They were short with pointed ears and if I didn't know better, I might have imagined that they were elves.

"Cyril. Clive. We've just heard the news. Come in," Nick opened the door.

The police elves looked awkward as they entered the hallway.

"Hot cocoa, boys? You'll be in for a long night, I'm sure," Mrs Claus offered.

"No thank you," one of the officers said in a surprisingly deep voice. "Mrs Claus, we're here to place you under house arrest. You must not leave Claus Cottage for any reason unless or until notified by Chief Superintendent Wiggles."

"What is this? Is this some kind of joke?" Nick asked. Even when stressed, his voice was a delight to listen to.

"I'm afraid not," an officer said.

"Well, explain it then. Please," Nick commanded.

The officers looked at each other awkwardly. "We're not allowed to discuss the investigation."

"Fine," Nick said. "I'll go and speak to Wiggles direct. Where is he? At the station?"

"Erm," the officers mumbled in unison.

"Where is he?"

"He's at the Polar Arms," one of the officers caved. The other shot him an annoyed glare.

"This is no time to be in the pub! Doesn't he realise there's a murderer on the loose?"

The officers shifted on the balls of their feet, then shot a glance at Mrs Claus.

"No! Are you fine gentlemen suggesting that I'm the killer?" Mrs Claus exclaimed.

"We can't discuss the investigation. We're going to take

up guard outside Claus Cottage, and any attempts to leave will result in you being taken to Candy Cane Custody."

"This is..." Nick began.

"Son, it's okay. These men are simply doing their job. The law applies to everyone equally. Even the Claus family have to follow the rules. It's okay, I'll stay right here. I have plenty to get on with. Now, how about that hot cocoa? You'll be cold out there."

"Sorry Mrs Claus, we've got strict instructions to not accept any food or drink from you."

"Oh, of course. Persephone was poisoned. Well, good thinking boys. You're absolutely right, if I was the killer, accepting my food or drink would be a silly thing to do. I can see why you two joined the force. Sharp as knives, aren't they Nick?"

Nick pursed his lips.

"Nicholas! Show some gratitude for our law enforcement. I raised you to have manners," Mrs Claus scolded him.

Nick let out a breath. "Thank you both for following your orders. I'm sure no officers relished the thought of this job. Placing Mrs Claus under house arrest! Ridiculous!"

"You're welcome. We'll be right outside," one officer said, and we all watched as Cyril and Clive ambled through the snow and took up their positions.

"I'll go and speak to Wiggles now, he's gone too far this time," Nick said as he opened an under stairs closet and pulled out a heavy coat.

"Don't be too hard on the man, Nick. If I'm a suspect, I have to be treated like any other person would be. Goodness me, poor Persephone. How awful. To just finish painting her nails and then be killed!"

Nick shook his head and trudged out of the cottage, past the police officers, and out of sight.

"He's a good boy," Mrs Claus said.

"Is he... I'm sorry, I know you have a lot on your mind right now. But, is he... is he Santa?" I asked. My cheeks flushed as I dared to ask the question aloud.

Mrs Claus burst into a grin. "You're a believer! I knew it!"

"Is that a yes?" I asked.

In truth, I'd never really stopped believing in Santa, in the magic of Christmas. As a big sister, it had been my job to help August continue to believe, and so even when my friends had decided that the big man wasn't real, I chose to continue believing. At some point, August must have stopped believing, but she never told me so. I guess we both wanted to help the other one experience the magic.

Mrs Claus simply looked at me and winked, but I saw the shadow of something darker in her expression.

"I'm sorry, here I am being all excited about Christmas, and you've just found out that a dear friend was murdered. Not to mention it looking like you're the prime suspect," I said.

"We must always remain excited about Christmas, dear. Everything else tends to sort itself out. And, trust me, I have a list of jobs to do around here. Some time to stay at home will come in quite handy!"

B y the time the door opened and Nick Claus returned home, Mrs Claus had called it a night and gone to bed. She'd given me a tour of Claus Cottage – the incredible kitchen with a real Aga, my guest room on the first floor, and a bathroom with an old fashioned claw-foot tub – and told me to make myself at home.

I'd stayed in the den, having already slept all of the tiredness out of my bones. Snowy curled up on the settee next to me and I absentmindedly stroked her.

"You're home," I called as Nick closed the door behind him. I didn't want to startle him so thought it best to announce my presence.

"Oh, hey there. Holly, right?" He came in the den and collapsed into a high-backed chair. There was ice hanging from his eyebrows.

"You look frozen. Can I return the favour and make you a drink?" I offered.

He began to shake his head but I was already up from the settee. If this family insisted on letting me stay the night, I could at least make myself useful.

I made two strong coffees and carried them back into the den. Snowy had moved from the settee on to Nick's lap and fallen right back to sleep.

"Are you okay? Are the police still out there?" I asked as I handed a coffee to Nick.

He looked up at me with concern in his eyes, then took a sip of the scalding liquid and didn't so much as wince at the temperature.

"They're still there, they will be all night. But, Holly, my mum isn't a murderer. I know you just met her, but I assure you you're safe here," Nick said.

"Oh, I know that. She's an absolute angel. She saved my life," I admitted. It hadn't occurred to me that I could be in danger around Mrs Claus.

"She did, huh?" Nick asked.

I relayed the story to Nick, his eyes wide as he listened.

"Wait. I've been with her all the time since 8pm. I'm her alibi!" I exclaimed.

Nick shook his head. "It would be good if that was the case."

"It is the case, I really have been with her," I insisted.

"Can I talk to you in confidence? I probably shouldn't talk to a stranger about the investigation, but I feel like I can trust you."

"You can," I said, as my stomach flipped.

"Wiggles told me that Persephone ate a poisoned mince pie. Not even a whole one, in fact. Dr Lancaster found the remaining cake on her desk."

"So whoever the killer was, they weren't physically with her when she died. That's smart," I said.

"Exactly. That's why you can't be my mum's alibi."

"Why is she the suspect then? I assumed it was because

she was the last person to see Persephone, when she took me to the surgery."

"That's not it. We do things a certain way here in Candy Cane Hollow. Everyone has their own things they're known for. Ginger Rumples, for example, she wins the ice sculpture competition every year. She has a very distinctive style. If you saw one of her sculptures, you'd know right away what you were looking at."

"Okay," I said, not really following what the relevance was.

"My mum's thing is mince pies. She bakes the best mince pies in town, and everyone knows a Mrs Claus mince pie just by looking at it."

"Let me guess. It was a Mrs Claus mince pie that poisoned Persephone?"

"That's what they're saying," Nick said.

"In that case, your mum's being framed. We have to help her."

"We?"

"She literally just saved my life, Nick. And I have nothing to get back home for anyway. Not that that's the point. The main thing is, she saved my life and now she needs help."

"Do you have a plan?"

"**N**o," I admitted.

Nick laughed, and there was that dimple again. Goodness me.

"I don't have a plan yet, but I'll think of one. We can work together. If you don't mind me staying here?"

"Of course not. The guest room's always made up ready for any surprise visitors."

"I didn't want to say, but Persephone said something along those lines. She said your mum's always bringing home waifs and strays."

Nick's expression darkened. "I'm sorry she said that to you. That's not the way it is."

"It's okay, I'm not upset by it. It seemed strange because she was so warm and friendly to your mum, but when your mum was in with Dr Lancaster, she was different."

"Shy?" Nick asked.

I laughed at that thought. "No, not in a shy way. She warned me off any ideas of settling down here. She told me there were no homes and no jobs free. It was odd. She seemed really territorial."

"That is odd. I like to think we're a really welcoming community here."

"You have been. You and your mum have been wonderful," I admitted.

Nick looked across at me and I felt my cheeks flush. To my surprise, his turned a similar shade of salmon. I looked away.

An awkward silence stretched out for a few moments before a ring of the doorbell broke it.

Nick jumped up and answered the door.

A woman walked in, planted a kiss on his cheek, and dropped a bag in the hallway.

I felt my stomach churn. Of course there was a female attached to the hunky Nick Claus.

"Ginger, this is Holly," Nick introduced.

I downed the rest of my coffee and staged a yawn. I didn't want to sit around and cramp their style.

"Oh, you're the famous Holly," Ginger crossed her arms and inspected me from the doorway. She was as red headed as her name suggested, with a smattering of wild freckles across her face.

"Holly, yes. Famous, no," I said with a weak smile. My own dark hair and office clothes felt very boring compared to her beauty.

"The town group chat was blowing up this evening about you," Ginger said with a grin. "But that's not why I'm here. Nick, are we going to just declare my win now? For the ice sculpture?"

"It hasn't been judged yet, and frankly it's not my priority right now," Nick answered.

"It seems a little insensitive to go through with the event, since my arch-rival is dead and one of the judges is under house arrest. Just declare me the winner and we can move on," Ginger said.

"Ginger, please. Now isn't the time. I won't be making any decisions like this tonight. Just go home and get some rest," Nick instructed. He held the door open and Ginger flounced into the night without a backward glance.

"I'm sorry," I offered. "It's probably a little odd for your girlfriend to walk in and see me here. I should call it a night."

"My girlfriend?" Nick asked, incredulously, as he sat back down.

"Ginger. You mean she isn't..."

"She's my oldest friend, that's why she seems so at home here. And why she tells me off as if it's second nature to her. She's got a good heart, she just hides it well."

"She didn't get on with Persephone?"

"Things have been strained between them ever since Persephone announced that she was entering the ice sculpture competition. That's been Ginger's gig for as long as I can remember. She lives to sculpt."

"Surely it wouldn't matter if Persephone entered, then? If Ginger really is that good, she'd still win," I said.

"It doesn't quite work that way. Persephone had to win, at everything. It was like an obsession with her. I have no idea why she decided to enter this year, but it was bad news for her friendship with Ginger. It was sad to see."

"Would Persephone have cheated to win?" I asked.

Nick shifted a little in his chair. "There are rumours, but that's all they are. I have no evidence either way."

"Nick, could Ginger be a suspect?" I asked, the words barely a whisper. I was a stranger to these people, and yet based on one quick conversation with Ginger I was suggesting she could be a murderer.

He groaned and buried his head in his hands. "I hate to say this, but I was just thinking the same thing."

9

I woke the next morning to the smell of batter and cinnamon and banana, and followed my nose down the stairs and into the kitchen.

Mrs Claus wore a red dress and a festive apron. When she turned and spotted me in the doorway, her face opened in such joy it was as though I was a long lost relative.

"Holly! What a delight you are! Do the clothes fit okay?" Mrs Claus asked as she looked me up and down.

I had been surprised to see a set of clothes, folded and smelling like cloves, on a hanger on the back of the door. The jeans and blouse were my size and the socks were made from bamboo. They were so soft I never wanted to trust my feet in anything else in the future.

"They're perfect. How did you know?"

"Oh, they're just spares I had around," Mrs Claus said. She batted the question away as if it was no big deal.

"Can I help? This smells wonderful," I said.

"No, no, sit yourself down. I love to have a house full of people. When it's just Nick and I we clunk around this big old house and it seems such a waste."

Speak of the very handsome devil, Nick appeared in the doorway. His hair looked uncombed, but adorable, and the slightest shadow of stubble covered his chin. I gulped as he pulled out the chair across from me and met my gaze.

"Good morning Holly, are you feeling better today?"

"Look at her, Nick! Of course she is! This is a woman right in the prime of good health," Mrs Claus exclaimed.

"I'm not sure about the prime of anything, but I'm feeling much better, thank you," I said with a laugh.

"I'm pleased to hear that," Nick said with a raised eyebrow. Was he flirting? No, of course not. I was being foolish. Blame the frost bite.

"I'll get out of your way this morning," I said.

Nick cocked his head to the side. "I thought you were hanging around and helping me with... that thing we discussed."

Mrs Claus clapped her hands together with glee.

"Mother..." Nick warned.

"What? Can't a mother be happy for her son? All I want is for you to be happy, Nick," Mrs Claus grinned.

Nick leaned in across the table until he was so close to me I wondered if I might spontaneously combust. He was about to say something when Mrs Claus appeared at the table with a plate in each hand.

"Oh, just look at the two of you. I knew last night that this would be the start of something marvellous," she gushed.

"Mother, have you forgot that you're under house arrest?"

"Like I said last night, it's a good opportunity to take care of some things around here. I have that 5,000 piece jigsaw that I still haven't finished from last Christmas! And I never get time to clean the good silver."

I tried to disguise my smile.

"Gilbert can do that," Nick said, then glanced at me. "He's our housekeeper."

I laughed. Nobody else did.

"You have a housekeeper?" I asked. I'd never heard of anyone having a housekeeper before. August had a cleaner, of course, and she spent hours cleaning the house in readiness for the cleaner arriving. That system didn't make much sense to me.

"It's not as grand as it sounds, dear," Mrs Claus said.

"This looks amazing, by the way," I said as I gazed dreamily at the French toast with maple syrup and caramelised bananas. My stomach grumbled.

"Mum's incredible in the kitchen," Nick said with a grin. He looked at his mother with pride.

"Why thank you, Nick."

"Where is Gilbert, anyway?"

"I gave him a few days off. He wanted to head across to Mistletoe Moor and see his second-cousin. You remember her, Nick? Such a darling girl."

Nick grunted in response, his mouth full of French toast.

"Mistletoe Moor?"

"It's a village across the river," Mrs Claus explained.

"Okay, I need to know what's going on here. I've been travelling on that motorway all of my life and I've never seen an exit for Candy Cane Hollow. Is this all... is it all some kind of elaborate joke?"

"Joke, dear?" Mrs Claus asked.

"Mrs Claus... Nick... Mistletoe Moor... elves! This can't all be real, can it?"

"I thought you said you believed," Mrs Claus reminded me.

"Well, I believe in the magic of Christmas, I guess.

Although my Christmas won't have much magic this year. Apart from this, of course, being here with you. But are you asking me to believe that you're really... that... is this the North Pole?"

Nick let out a laugh. "The North Pole was a little too frosty. Not to mention impractical. We're 40 minutes from London here. It's much more effective."

"Are you saying that you used to be at the North Pole? Hold on. Okay, I'm just going to ask. Are you Santa?"

Nick's cheeks flushed.

"He is, dear. He's the most wonderful Santa. You should see him in the suit he wears on Christmas Eve!" Mrs Claus practically squealed.

"I'm not the most wonderful Santa, mum. That was dad," Nick said, and squeezed his mother's hand.

Mrs Claus' eyes filled with tears and I felt my heart fill with a premature sadness that I'd have to leave Candy Cane Hollow soon.

"I can't believe it," I murmured.

"It's a shock for people. That's why the exit's hidden. We don't generally have people here, but mum just had to get you to a doctor. I hope the surprise isn't too much for you."

"No, no... it's probably just what I need. A chance to believe again. So, wait, those police officers, they really are elves?"

"Cyril and Clive? They sure are. You'll see plenty of elves around town."

"Persephone was a regular person, like us?"

"She was. The Hyde-Barkers have been around for generations. There are seven regular human families here. Family names, I mean. It can get a little confusing."

Mrs Claus silently reached for our empty plates and busied herself with filling the sink with warm, soapy water.

"Can I do that? Please? It's the least I can do after your hospitality," I offered, already halfway up out of my seat.

"Nonsense! You carry on talking to Nick. He's a very good conversationalist, you know," Mrs Claus said.

"Mother..." Nick warned.

"She's wonderful," I gushed as I returned to my seat.

Nick wiped his mouth with a handkerchief emblazoned with tiny cartoon Christmas trees. "I need to get on with things. Do you want to join me, Holly? We can work on that thing we discussed."

"I'd love to!"

I f I expected Nick to travel by sleigh, I would have been disappointed. He escorted me through the cottage, out into an attached garage, where he opened the passenger door to a very regular-looking 4x4 and gestured for me to climb in.

He must have seen my puzzled expression because he asked what I was thinking.

"No sleigh?" I asked.

He cocked his head back and laughed. "I try to give the reindeers a break before Christmas Eve. Christmas Magic goes so far, but it's still a big night for them. They're pretty tired afterwards."

"I'm sure they are," I said. The whole thing felt surreal, and maybe I was dreaming it all or it was some weird side effect of the frost bite, but I wanted to believe. I was sick of being so grown-up and practical and cynical. When did I get so cynical?

"What are you hoping for this Christmas?"

"Shouldn't you know that, Santa?" I teased.

He grimaced. "Call me Nick, please. I hear Santa and

think you're talking to my father. And I would only know what you wanted if you'd made a list, which you haven't."

I gasped. "How do you know that?"

"It's part of the whole Santa gig. You really should write one," Nick said as the garage door opened. He waved at Cyril and Clive as we drove by.

The sight of Candy Cane Hollow in the daylight was breathtaking. A blanket of snow covered the ground, and in between the ornate lampposts, the village had 12 feet tall candy canes. Every single house we passed featured elaborate decorations and lights, and a field we passed was filled with families enjoying snowball fights and making snowmen.

I grinned as we slowed by another field and a herd of reindeer turned and began to approach.

"The reindeer!" I exclaimed.

Nick waved at the animals then continued the drive. Every person we passed waved and smiled at us. Their neighbourliness was such a refreshing change to see.

We pulled up outside a grand building that featured a statue of a toy soldier at either end. A huge sign atop the building read Santa HQ.

"This place looks incredible," I said as we climbed out of the vehicle.

"Welcome to Tinker Town. This is the commercial hub of Candy Cane Hollow, I guess. And this is the factory. Let me show you around," Nick said.

As soon as we approached the building, a young female elf held the door open. She had a clipboard in her other hand and took a breath as we entered the building.

"Good morning Santa, and unknown female. Here's the order of the day. There's a slight issue with Zone 2 – Hermione fell asleep at the belt again so let's just say that things are backed up there. Everything is smooth in Lots for Tots, but let's just say that's because I've personally been supervising Wilma for the last week. More letters came in today, I've sifted through and organised the ones I can. Johnny in Pennsylvania is trouble again. He wants a monster truck. A real full-size one. Blitzen still hasn't stopped moaning about that life-sized king penguin cuddly he had last year. And then..."

"Holly, this is my assistant Mitzy," Nick explained.

"... the thing with Hermione falling asleep. I've turned the Christmas music up to volume 10 by her work station. Shouldn't happen again! And..."

"There's more?" Nick joked.

"Everyone's asking about Persephone and those elves outside Claus Cottage. Rumour has it that Mrs Claus poisoned her and Wiggles will be sending her to Candy Cane Custody just as soon as he can organise it."

"Well..." Nick didn't seem to give anything away.

"Goodness gumdrops! It's true! I was ho-ho-hoping there was another explanation."

"How many people know?" Nick asked.

Mitzy made a show of looking from side to side, then whispered, "Everyone! Even old Bum McGhee mentioned something, and he barely knows what year it is. Mrs Claus really killed Persephone?"

"What? Of course not!" Nick exclaimed.

Mitzy looked a little disappointed. "But the police..."

"...are investigating. And we all know that rumours don't help the police do their job. I expect you, Mitzy, to remind people of that if needed. Are we clear?"

"Yes, Santa. Of course. I mean, murder in Candy Cane Hollow is terrible, but if it had to be anyone, it's not much surprise it was her."

"Why do you say that?" I asked.

Mitzy looked me up and down. "Santa, permission to speak to an outsider?"

"Of course," he rolled his eyes.

"Are you sure? Because..."

"This is Holly. She's my guest. She's to be treated as such."

"Hmm, well I guess. What was the question? I struggle a little with accents."

I stifled a laugh. Mitzy was frustrating but somehow adorable. "I asked why you said it's not a surprise it was Persephone who was killed?"

"You didn't have the pleasure of meeting her, I take it. Persephone was one of those people who really had her nose in everyone's business. Let's see. If she saw you hang your Christmas lights only to then switch them on and blow the power, she'd stand by and snicker."

"I see," I said. If that was enough of a reason to kill someone, I should have become a serial killer a long time ago.

"Now, Santa, did you make a decision about where to host the Christmas party?"

Nick grimaced. "Isn't that a little distasteful with all that's going on?"

"It's been a rough year. Christmas lists have increased in length by 27% on last year, and we never really did replace the Winkle brothers. Those two were powered by some 300-elf-power engine. Everyone needs a celebration. A reminder that Santa appreciates the hard work."

"Okay, I get that. Go ahead and book whichever you think is best. Now, I need to speak to Holly. I'm DND for the next hour."

"As you wish," Mitzy said.

We had reached Nick's office and Mitzy closed the door

on her way out. The office was large, very plush, and had a wonderful view. The snow-covered scene looked heavenly and I didn't know how I'd achieve anything other than sipping hot chocolate and looking out of the window if it was my workspace.

It was clear that Nick didn't have that luxury. Being Santa was a full-time, full-scale operation.

"Holly, were you serious that you could help my mum?" Nick asked. His tone was serious and I realised he must have been building up the courage to ask the question.

"Of course! It's the least I can do."

"And your expertise? What are you? Was it a lawyer or a cop, I don't remember."

My cheeks flushed. "Oh, no, nothing like that. I'm just a... well, I'm not even employed right now. I was driving home from my last day of work. Maternity cover."

"But you think you might be able to help clear her name?"

"Well, I'm willing... and if you don't mind me cramping your style by sticking around, I really have nothing at all to get home for. Not even a houseplant."

"That's awful. Everyone should have something waiting for them to get home at night."

"Well, yeah... anyway. I can get a hotel. I wouldn't expect to stay at Claus Cottage."

"Nonsense, have you noticed how much my mum likes you? There aren't any hotels here, anyway, since we don't have visitors. You're welcome to stay with us as long as you want. Selfishly, it would be a huge help to me. This is my busiest time of year and there's no way I can have Christmas ready and help my mum. It's an impossible choice."

"It's fine. An outsider's perspective might even be a benefit. But I do need some information so I can get started. Can we run through things now?"

"Of course, I'm all yours," Nick said. My stomach spasmed.

"It doesn't seem like Mitzy liked Persephone. Were they enemies?"

Nick furrowed his brow. "I don't know about things like that. The elves kind of idolise me. Gosh, that's embarrassing to admit. It's not just me, either, it's whoever the current Santa is. They all snap to attention when they see me, and whatever they chat about when I'm not in the room, it all stops when I walk in."

"That makes sense. You're their boss, they're not going to be that relaxed with you."

"Boss? Ugh, I hate that word."

"Mitzy seemed at ease with you," I prompted.

"She's the exception. She has no filter. Whatever she thinks, she says. Which is a good thing when you're surrounded by yes-elves."

"But no grudge between her and Persephone that you know about?"

"No. I know very little about Persephone, actually. The most I heard about her was that she was like a guard dog over at the surgery. She made it hard to speak to Dr Lancaster, apparently. But I can't imagine anyone killing her because of that."

"And the mince pie thing. What's going on with that? It's like your mother's speciality or something?"

"Exactly that. She bakes mince pies for the whole town."

"Do other people bake them?"

"I guess. But mum's are the best. And I guess nobody wants to offend Mrs Claus by copying. It's just her thing. But it's not like she's tried to stop anyone else baking some too."

"Okay. Nick, if you had the time, where would you start? Who would you talk to first?"

Nick gazed out of the window and considered the question. "Dr Lancaster, maybe? He found her. Maybe he saw something."

11

I bid a reluctant farewell to Nick and assured him that I would be fine exploring on foot. I wanted some fresh air and the chance to get an understanding of the layout of the place.

Frequent signposts pointed the way to the various parts of town; Tinker Town, Mistletoe Moor, Poinsettia Precinct, Claus Cottage.

I followed the roads until I recognised some shops from the night before. It had occurred to me that the doctor's surgery may be closed, but to my relief the door was open.

I walked in without knocking, in case Dr Lancaster was with a patient.

I took a chair in the small waiting area and made myself look at the reception desk. Persephone had been there the night before, warning me away from getting too comfortable in Candy Cane Hollow, and now she was dead and I was staying around at the request of Santa. I wondered what she'd make to it all.

I was pulled out of my thoughts by a noise from the adjoining room. It was a pathetic noise, like an injured animal, and I felt my heart beat frantically as I wondered whether the killer had returned.

I glanced around the room for a weapon and grabbed the best thing I could see, then pushed the door open and entered – with the shatterproof ruler held up above my head.

Dr Lancaster took his head from his hands and looked at me in confusion. I looked from left to right. He was alone in the room, and his eyes looked awful red and puffy.

"You have an appointment?" He asked, his voice shaky.

I considered how best to play the situation and decided to follow his lead. "You asked me to pop by so you could check the frost bite?"

He seemed utterly lost, then a flash of recognition crossed his face. "You're that woman! You came in here with Mrs Claus!"

"That's right. I'm Holly. Is now a bad time?"

"It's an awful time."

"I'm sorry. Can I do anything to help?"

"Can you turn back time?" Dr Lancaster held his arms out, palms up. I sat down in the seat across the table from him.

"I wish. That would sure come in handy. What's happened?" I asked. Since I didn't have a better idea, I decided to play dumb.

"Persephone's gone," he croaked.

"Your receptionist?"

"My... my Percy."

A nickname. Interesting. "Did she make it home last night? She was here when Mrs Claus brought me in."

The doctor shook his head. "I found her out there."

"That must have been awful. I know you're a doctor, but..."

"Doctors don't usually go about their personal life discovering dead bodies!"

"Exactly. What did you do?"

"I tried to resuscitate her, of course. I checked her pulse. I thought she'd fallen asleep at first, worried that she was ill or working too hard. Well, not working too hard. She'd been too distracted for that."

"Distracted?"

"Most people here find it hard to concentrate so close to Christmas. I'm an outsider, I came for the job and I've never really understood the festive cheer."

"It was just an annual distraction, then? Or did Persephone have anything in particular on her mind?"

"No," he snapped.

"Not the ice sculpting competition?"

"I don't talk about that nonsense. Not with staff."

"She seemed to be very focused on winning it but apparently she'd never entered before. Is that a little odd?"

"She was always trying her hand at new things," Dr Lancaster said.

"Really? Like what?"

"What is this? Why are you asking all of these questions?"

"I'm just nosey, sorry," I said.

"Do you want me to give you a once-over or not?" Dr Lancaster asked, and I was reminded on the ruse I'd used to get into his room.

"Well, I don't know. I feel fine. I only stopped by because you said I should."

He frowned and rose from his chair, grabbed his medical bag. He listened to my heartbeat, took my temperature and asked me to hold my hands out.

"Did you call an ambulance?"

"Of course. Doctors have to call in a death like anyone else. It was already too late, though. She'd had a bite of that mince pie with her first coffee of the day. She never could resist a sweet treat."

"Where did the mince pie come from? You haven't eaten one, have you?" I asked.

"Like I say, I'm not as festive as the other people here. I was never won over by the mince pie fetish."

"Lucky for you," I gave a weak smile.

"Well, you seem fine. And I can say that because I'm a doctor! The paramedics insisted on checking, you know. Checking if she was alive. As if I'd falsely declare someone dead! I'm a doctor, I told them."

"I guess they have to be sure," I shrugged.

"I was sure! Why wouldn't they believe me? It was an insult and I'll be making a formal complaint. I was prescribing folic acid tablets when their mothers were pregnant with them, and then they turn up and second guess me!"

"It's an emotional time. Should you be here today?"

"Where else would I be?"

"Erm, at home maybe? With your..."

"...family? There is no family! Not now. This is all I have."

"Do you know who might have wanted to hurt her?"

Dr Lancaster's eyes found me and a blob of a tear escaped and plopped on his desk. He shook his head.

"You knew her well it seems. Is there anything you can think of that might help?"

Dr Lancaster scoffed. "We worked together for many years, of course I knew her well. Probably better than most. Nobody could want to hurt Percy. Nobody. Nobody in their right mind."

There came a soft knock on the door behind me.

A short, elderly elf stood with a walking stick. "Sorry, Dr, I've come for my blood results. I didn't know as you'd be open."

"I'll leave you to it," I said, and squeezed past the elf in the doorway.

As I left the room, I noticed that Christmas music played quietly from somewhere within. I wondered whether it was on a timer or whether Dr Lancaster had come in and gone about his normal morning routine on auto pilot.

12

I left Dr Lancaster's office but hung around in the reception area.

Persephone's desk had been cleared. Even her computer screen and keyboard were gone. I went around to the back of her desk and opened the top drawer.

Persephone, it turned out, was a neat freak. Her top drawer housed four pens, laid out in a perfect row, a stapler, a hole punch, a notepad, and a small diary.

I pulled out the diary and flicked through its pages. Most were blank.

On today's date, Persephone had written: *ICE SCULP-TURE QUEEN*. She'd even stuck in a crown sticker.

Well that was a little presumptuous.

On Christmas Day, she'd written: *LUNCH @ CLAUS COTTAGE*

And on the notes page right at the end of the book were two scribbled lines of writing.

The first said *Dr L?!* in blue pen but had been crossed out in a red pen. The second, in red pen, said *wedding?????????*

I took a deep breath and knocked on Dr Lancaster's door. He looked up at me and the old elf turned in her chair.

"I'm so sorry, excuse me. I don't know where my manners are at. I'd like to go and give my thoughts to Persephone's family. Her fiancé? Where could I find him?"

"Fiance? There's no fiancé! She were always looking for the next best thing, she were," the patient said with a laugh.

Dr Lancaster pursed his lips. "She lived with her mother at Pine Cone Cottage. Right at the end of the High Street, you can't miss it."

I thanked the doctor and apologised again for interrupting him, then set off in search of Pine Cone Cottage.

Dr Lancaster was right, it stood at the very top of the High Street. It was a tiny building really, but incredibly picturesque. A woman with a rather bulbous nose had appeared at the window before I'd made it down the postage stamp of a garden to knock on the door.

"And you are?"

"My name's Holly Wood, I'm here to..."

"Holly Wood? As in glitz and glamour, films and celebs? Hollywood?"

"Yes, that's exactly right," I said with a smile.

"Well, I thought I had it rough. I guess it's true what they say. There really is someone else who has it worse. Holly Wood. What a name. You coming in?"

"Please," I said, and followed the woman into the cottage. I had to duck to get in the doorway. Inside, there was a Christmas tree in the hallway and another in the lounge. Logs burned away in the fireplace.

A cinnamon candle flickered on the windowsill.

"I take it you're here to pay your respects?"

"Yes," I said, startled.

"You're the fourteenth person today. Funny how nobody

visited when she was alive. I'm sorry, my name's Moira. I'm her mum. Or am I? Do I say I was her mum? Ooh, there's so much to learn. Well, your respects are paid. Thank you very much."

"It must be awful to lose a daughter in such a tragic way," I said.

"Death by mince pie? Don't know whether it's a tragedy or a comedy!"

"Erm... quite. You said she didn't have many visitors? Before she died?"

"Only that doctor. I told him to stop hassling her after hours. Surely nothing can be that urgent after work?"

I knew first hand that the medical profession was one where things probably could be that urgent after work, but didn't say so.

"It sounds like she was very good at her work," I said.

"Yes, when she set her mind to something she achieved it. She was a real asset to that doctor. He's great with his prescriptions but you should see his filing system. I worry for him. I don't know how he'll cope without her."

"And you? How will you cope without her? I'm sorry, it's just... awful generous of you to worry about how her employer will manage!"

Moira's cheeks flushed. "I guess it hasn't sunk in for me yet. Worrying about everyone else is another way of keeping busy. I even thought about heading across to the surgery and offering the doctor a hand myself, but I can't do that until tomorrow."

I raised an eyebrow quizzically.

"It's the ice sculpting competition today. Persephone wouldn't forgive me if I missed it."

"It's going ahead?"

"Oh, yes. Mrs Claus sent a message offering to cancel the

whole thing, but I couldn't let that happen. Too many people have worked hard for it all. I'll be there cheering them on, in her memory."

"You really are incredibly generous. I don't know that I could be as warm hearted as you are. Good for you. I'm sure it will help when the investigation is finished, too, and you know who did it. Do you have any ideas?"

"Ideas of what? Who poisoned that mince pie? Well, no. I know that Mrs Claus is the first thought, but there's no way she would hurt anyone. She's such a dear. Persephone really looked up to her."

I scanned the room and saw a framed photograph on the wall. A girl, presumably Persephone, sat on a bearded Santa's lap.

"That's the old Father Christmas. He was the best. No offence to Nick, he does a good job for a young guy. But his dad really put the merry in a merry Christmas."

"Percy really loved Christmas, didn't she? It's kind of particularly cruel that it would be something so festive – a mince pie! – used against her," I murmured.

Moira frowned a little. "My daughter was obsessed with Santa, like most kids are. She just never grew out of it. She loved all things Christmas, she filled her life with everything to do with the holidays."

"Like ice sculpting?"

"Well, that was fairly new," Moira admitted.

"What made her get into it? It sounds like she already had a lot going on without picking up a new hobby."

"Oh! That's easy. It's this year's prize. She had her sights set on winning," Moira said.

So it was all about the competitiveness with Persephone. She'd wanted to win.

"Was she good? Do you think she might have won?" I asked.

Moira laughed. "Of course she would! Anything she set her mind to, she accomplished."

I smiled and said my goodbyes, then saw myself out of the tiny little cottage. As I closed the gate behind me, I could see Moira back in the window, looking out.

I hadn't got far when my phone rang. The electronic jingle made me jump and also slip on the snow.

I glanced at the screen and saw it was my sister calling.

"August? Hey!" I said as the skies opened and more snow began to fall. I held my hand out and watched the snowflakes gather and then disappear on my palm.

"Hey, so I need to ask you a question," my sister didn't sound like her normal serene self. She was out of breath. Plus, she never forgot to make pleasantries before getting to the point.

"Is everything okay?"

"No, it's really not. And why aren't you at home? I've rang your landline three times already. You never go anywhere other than work and I know yesterday was your last day, I had it marked in my Erin Condren," she said. Of course. Every single thing was logged and colour-coded in August's planner. I wondered if I had a whole colour devoted to me, or whether I was part of a larger miscellaneous group of things to be noted.

"Yeah, sorry, I'm erm... I'm out," I said dumbly.

"The thing is Holly, it's Jeb."

"Goodness gumdrops, is he okay?" I asked.

"What did you just say? Are you making fun of me right now?" August snapped. August never snapped. Things must be really bad, and I'd slipped in a Candy Cane Hollow colloquialism without even realising.

"No, I'm sorry, of course I'm not making fun of you. What's happened?"

August took a deep breath and I pictured her, standing in her recently refurbished kitchen, probably stirring something on the Aga as she spoke to me.

"Do you think we were completely harmed by screen time as kids?"

I let out the first rumour of a laugh, then stopped myself. "Harmed? You mean by watching TV?"

"Screen time! Any screen time. Has it ruined your life? Is that why you're still single and have no life outside of work?"

"Oh my gosh," I muttered.

"Please be honest with me, because I need to know how much to freak out right now," August said.

"Well, I've never really considered myself to be too much of a failure. Not until this call, anyway. I might not be as settled as you, but I like to think I'm kind and I work hard. I donate my old clothes to the charity shop. I'm not totally ruined, maybe?"

"I'm not saying you are, I'm just asking the question. I mean, maybe our parents set us up to fail, in which case it wouldn't even be your fault. I remember we came home from school and the first thing we did was watch TV."

"Is there a reason this is on your mind right now, sis?" I asked.

She made a choked noise and I realised she was close to tears. "I put Jeb down for his nap today, like normal, and then I checked my planner and I had a few calls to make, and then I wanted to experiment with a trifle recipe. Time just got away from me, and I didn't realise how long he'd been down for. I did think at some point it was a nice long nap, a good chance to get some chores done. I should have gone up to him then and just checked! But I didn't, until I heard him laugh."

"Okay..."

"Don't hate me, Holly, please. I went up to him and he was in his cot with my tablet! He must have rolled onto it and switched it on, and it went right back to what I'd been watching that morning."

"What had you been watching?" I asked. I wondered if I would be morally bound to ring Social Services if she said porn. Not that I could imagine my sister doing that. But still.

"I don't usually do this, Holly, not with Jeb around, but I was watching the news," August said. I let out a breath I didn't realise I'd been holding.

"The news? You're calling me in a panic because of the news?"

"I checked the baby monitor. It was seven minutes and twelve seconds of the news. He's seemed fine since."

"You mean he hasn't started speaking in headline format?" I teased.

"He doesn't talk yet, he's only a baby..."

"I know. That was a joke."

"This is no time for joking! Should I ring the doctor? Or maybe take him straight to A&E. They could do a brain scan or something, perhaps," August said.

I sighed. She was neurotic, but she was my sister and I loved her.

"Sis, he'll be fine. When we were babies, our mum was dipping dummies in whisky to get us to sleep. You haven't ruined his life by accidentally allowing him a little screen time."

I heard her exhale and the sound made me smile. We might not speak all the time, but I'd been the person she'd phoned for help. That meant a lot.

"Thank you. I know I can be a little crazy at times. It's good to hear your voice."

"Yours too," I admitted.

"It's not too late to join us for Christmas, you know. We'll have plenty enough food. I'm doing flavoured butters!"

"It sounds amazing," I said. It really did. August didn't do anything by halves.

I looked out at the scene on Candy Cane Hollow's High Street as I listened to my sister describe the complicated feast she had planned for the big day. The snow was falling and right before my eyes, regular people like me and elves with pointed ears mingled around as they carried out their business. A group of carol singers were stopping outside every shop and singing a shop for the busy shopkeepers, and even the garbage collectors whistled festive tunes as they collected rubbish.

"You guys have this Christmas to yourselves. I'm going to stay where I am for now," I said. A thrill rang through me as I said the words. I'd stumbled across this magical place, and I wanted to spend more time exploring it.

Even if there was a murderer on the loose.

13

By the time I returned to Claus Cottage, it was approaching lunch time and the smell from the kitchen was incredible.

I poked my head around the door, expecting to see Mrs Claus, but in her place stood a tall, slender elf in a dark green topcoat and tails.

"Hello!" I exclaimed.

The elf turned and looked me up and down, then rested his wooden spoon in a tiny dish that looked designed for that exact purpose. I wondered if August had one of those. If not, I should buy her one.

"You must be Holly. I'm Gilbert. Delighted to meet you. Are you hungry?"

I let out a laugh. "I am, actually. But I wanted to speak to Mrs Claus. Is she around?"

He glanced at a very ostentatious watch on his slender wrist. "She'll be down in precisely six minutes. Her nap time's almost over."

"She gets nap time and lunch prepared for her?" I asked with wide eyes.

"She gets everything she needs and more. She *is* Mrs Claus. This whole place would fall apart without her."

"Really? Even with Nick around? Isn't he the, erm, face of Christmas?"

"That's exactly it. Nick's focused on the Christmas experience for everyone out there. It's Mrs Claus who oversees the running of Candy Cane Hollow."

"And if Nick got married?" I asked, then cleared my throat and tried to look natural.

Gilbert smiled to himself. "The new Mrs Claus would assist. Consider it on the job training. Until the time came for Mrs Claus herself to pass on the baton."

"Wow. It's like the Royal Family."

"Exactly. The Clauses are our royalty and we all admire them greatly. I've served the Claus family since I was twenty years old. I devoted my whole childhood to learning the trade. It was my biggest dream and it's been my highest honour."

"It doesn't seem like everyone admires the Claus family. I take it you've heard about Persephone? And Mrs Claus being under house arrest?"

Gilbert frowned. "It's awful business. But I'm sure that things will sort themselves out! And it's very important that Mrs Claus isn't above the law."

"You think she should just stay home and not fight it? For such a loyal elf, you seem pretty relaxed with just trusting that it will all work itself out." I said.

"What choice do I have? I can cook and clean and take care of people but I'm no detective. Anyway, Mrs Claus told me that you're going to sort it all out."

A chuckle came from behind us.

Mrs Claus stood there with Cyril and Clive on either side of her small frame.

"That's not exactly what I said, Gilbert. Now, these hard-working officers have been standing outside for hours. Can we get them some hot cocoa and a spot of lunch?"

"Yes, ma'am, coming right up," Gilbert busied himself with grabbing a big saucepan and adding milk to warm.

I watched Mrs Claus closely. Feeding and taking care of the very officers who were holding her under house arrest?! She was a better person than me, that was for sure. I'd have been tempted to turn the heating up high then stand in the window and watch them shiver outside.

"Cyril, how's your dad doing?"

"He's fully recovered now, thank you Mrs Claus," the officer answered.

"That must be such a relief for you all. And Clive, how's Rocket?"

"Oh, man, he's so fast! I take him out for a run as often as work allows. He's grown too!"

"I'll bet! Holly, Rocket is Clive's new reindeer. He's a very handsome chap," Mrs Claus explained. She gave me a smile that reached her eyes and made them sparkle, and I found myself doing the same back. Why should she have any ill will towards these police officers? They were just following orders and they probably felt awful about it.

"Sounds great. I don't have any pets. Not even a house-plant," I made my regular joke but it didn't quite land. I realised as I said the words just how empty my life back home was. I should reach out to August more. Make more effort with friends. Maybe even try the dating app that several colleagues had told me about, although the thought of choosing a partner based on a single filtered photo and a few key words seemed totally uninspiring.

"I don't blame you. They all take up time. My house is overflowing with elves, there's no room for pets," Cyril said.

Gilbert placed a mug of hot cocoa in front of each of us and the officers wrapped their hands around them to help them warm up. Their earlier reluctance to eat or drink while on guard had disappeared.

"Oh, my house isn't overflowing with anything. I live alone," I said.

Cyril and Clive eyed each other as if each hoping the other would translate.

"That's wonderful! A strong, independent woman, that's what you are Holly," Mrs Claus dived in and saved the moment.

"Thank you," I said as a blush took over my cheeks.

She was right. I was strong and independent, and for years living alone had been a point of pride for me. I was happy in my own company. If I had a bill, I paid it myself. If my car broke, I took it to the garage and dealt with the mechanic on my own. I'd even learned a little DIY over the years.

But lately I'd found myself yearning for a companion, someone to share the highs and the lows of daily life with.

"So, gentlemen, how's the investigation going? Do you have any more insight into poor Persephone's death?" Mrs Claus asked.

I waited for the officers to clam up and refuse to talk to her since she was apparently their prime suspect, but they simply shrugged their shoulders.

"We've not heard anything," Cyril admitted.

"Well, I'm sure Chief Superintendent Wiggles is doing a fine job. He'll want to interview me at some point, I'd imagine?"

"Oh yes," Clive said, although he looked anything but certain.

"What is the evidence against Mrs Claus?" I asked.

"Well, it's erm..."

"It's the mince pie, isn't it? Wiggles thinks it's one of mine," Mrs Claus said.

"Have you seen it?" I asked.

Mrs Claus shook her head.

"I've got a photo of it," Clive said. He reached into the inside pocket of his huge Candy Cane Constabulary coat and pulled out what looked like a standard issue mobile phone, complete with a bulky protective case. He thumbed his way through his camera roll and then slid the device across the table.

Mrs Claus and I both leaned in.

The image was a close-up of the mince pie I'd noticed on Persephone's desk. A bite had been taken from it, revealing the mince-meat filling inside. It looked delicious and I began to salivate a little.

"It's just a mince pie," I said.

"It's mine," Mrs Claus admitted.

14

"Mrs Claus, can you help me with something? Urgently? Please," I said, and darted up from the kitchen table.

Mrs Claus apologised to Cyril and Clive and followed me into the den.

"What's wrong, dear?" She asked, her eyes full of concern as I closed us into the room.

"You've just said that the mince pie is yours!" I hissed.

She blinked at me. "Well it is."

"Okay. First of all, how can you be so sure. And second, those are police officers. You can't just say things like that to them. They'll use it as evidence against you!"

"Oh!" Mrs Claus clasped her hands over her mouth as she grinned.

"What?"

"You're very good at this, dear! Are you sure you're not a detective? It never occurred to me not to say it, because it's true. Honesty's the best policy, right?"

"Not always," I mumbled.

"Shall I go no comment? I've heard about that on the TV before. How exciting!"

"No, you don't need to go no comment. You're not being interviewed. But if you're going to invite Cyril and Clive into the house, you need to remember that their job is to gather evidence against you. Don't make it easy for them."

"Don't make it easy for them. Right, I've got it. Thank you so much, dear. It's such a help knowing you're looking out for me," Mrs Claus reached for my hand and gave it a squeeze.

"Are you really sure that mince pie is one of yours?" I asked.

Mrs Claus nodded. "Absolutely. It has the Claus Crest on it."

"And there's no way that someone else could copy that?"

"Oh, no. It's against the law to imitate another family's crest," Mrs Claus appeared genuinely shocked at the suggestion.

"Well, murder is also illegal so I'm guessing the killer might not have been put off by that."

"Good point. But, no, the Claus Crest is the most elaborate of them all. It couldn't be copied," Mrs Claus explained.

"So your mince pie really did have poison in? Is that a likely conclusion to reach?"

"A devastating one, but it's fair. Yes, it appears that my mince pie somehow killed poor Persephone."

"And we have to figure out how. Could someone have interfered with the ingredients? Added something to the mincemeat jar, perhaps?"

Mrs Claus gasped. "There is no mincemeat jar! I create that mix by hand and the secret ingredient is love, not poison. Do you realise that they've been around the whole town recalling my mince pies? Warning people not to eat them? It's dreadful. A Christmas without my mince pies. I never thought I'd see the day."

"Of course. They'd have to do that. Have they tested them?"

"I believe so. I'm only hearing what's on the news. They haven't found poison in any others."

"No, I didn't expect they would. That means it was a targeted attack, which is easier to get to the bottom of."

"It is?" Mrs Claus asked.

I nodded. "Most murder victims are killed by someone close to them."

"That's awful. Did your travels this morning reveal anything helpful?"

"I don't know. I visited Dr Lancaster and then I went to see Persephone's mum."

"How is Moira? I wanted to send a poinsettia, but I didn't know if it was appropriate."

I thought back to Moira's support for the Claus family. "You could send one. She made it very clear she doesn't believe you're the killer."

"I'll do it right after lunch. Speaking of lunch, we should get back. It isn't proper to have guests and leave them unattended."

"One last thing. Was Persephone engaged? I found her diary and it mentioned a wedding."

Mrs Claus considered the question. "Goodness, no, I'm pretty sure she was single. Maybe it was someone else's wedding?"

"I guess so," I said, and we returned to the kitchen.

The smell hit me again and my stomach rumbled a little. I'd always thought that eating a big breakfast made me feel hungrier for the rest of the day somehow.

"Perfect timing," Gilbert said. He spooned the chilli into

bowls with a flourish, added a sprig of coriander to each, and began to serve.

"This looks incredible," I said.

Gilbert opened the oven door and pulled out a fresh loaf of sourdough, which he sliced and lathered with butter. This place was not good for my waistline.

We ate in silence, the officers hungrily spooning the meal into their mouths without even blowing it. Mrs Claus had a daintier way of eating, and even Gilbert pulled up a seat and joined in.

We'd virtually finished when the front door burst open, boots stomped in the hallway, and Nick appeared. He grinned at the sight of us all eating together.

Gilbert jumped up from his own seat and offered to serve a portion for Nick.

"Sit down, I'll help myself," Nick insisted and I watched as he manoeuvred his way around the kitchen space in trousers that nicely showed off the shape of his legs.

"We'll leave you to it," Cyril and Clive spoke in unison. Their bowls were so clean it was hard to tell that anyone had eaten from them.

"Nice to see you both. Come and knock if you need another hot cocoa," Mrs Claus said.

"We sure appreciate it, thank you. Shall we wash these?"

"Absolutely not," Gilbert said in his clipped voice, offended by the idea that someone else would wash dishes in his kitchen.

"If you're sure. We'll be on our way."

The officers left and Nick sat across from me. I tried to concentrate on the food in front of me.

"You find your way around town okay?" Nick asked.

"I did. It was nice to explore on foot. How was your morning?"

"Busy, but it always is this time of year."

"Do you really deliver all of the presents in one night?" I asked.

Gilbert's fork clattered to the table. "You really are new here, huh?"

I laughed. "I'm still adjusting to it all, I guess."

"It's okay. It is a lot to take in. The world has grown so rational now. It's like people will only believe if there's a scientific equation that explains it all," Nick said.

"And is there?" I asked.

Nick laughed. His dimple winked at me. "No, there's no science that explains the magic of Christmas."

"How about the magic of poison getting inside a home baked mince pie?" I asked.

"Not possible," Gilbert said.

"Not possible?"

"I buy all of the food for Claus Cottage and this kitchen is cleaned every single day. Several times a day!"

"Nobody's suggesting that the pie killed her because it was baked in a dirty kitchen," Nick said with a smile.

"Trust me Nicholas, if I don't let dirt in this kitchen I certainly don't let poison in,' Gilbert sat straighter in his chair.

"Could it be some kind of accident? Rat poison or something..."

Gilbert gasped. "All of our chemical products are sealed in a container. I'm the only one who has the key."

"You really should let me have a key," Mrs Claus said.

"I've failed as a housekeeper if you feel the need to reach those cleaning products yourself, Mrs Claus. I'll just hang up my tails now and be done with it."

Nick caught my eye and gave me a smile that sent a jolt

of electric through my body. There was more than Christmas magic going on, I'd bet an advent calendar on it.

Just my luck, the first eligible bachelor I'd met in years was Santa himself.

"Gilbert, that's not what I'm suggesting! I just think in case of emergency – what if the cookies and milk slip out of my hand one night. Or illness! What if you get sick?"

"I'm at your service 24 hours a day, every day. That's the oath I swore and I don't plan on breaking it. I took those words seriously."

"I know you did, dear. Forget I said anything. We're very lucky to have you," Mrs Claus said.

Nick glanced at his watch across the table and let out a sigh. "I need to go. The ice sculpture competition's about to start. Are you sure you're happy for me to go?"

"Of course! The show must go on. I have plenty of things to keep me busy here," Mrs Claus gushed.

"Like cleaning your own kitchen," Gilbert grumbled.

We all laughed. Gilbert was a hard worker but he sure seemed dramatic.

"Fancy coming with me, Holly? I know this isn't any regular Christmas, but these competitions are really impressive."

"Sure!" I exclaimed, a little too eagerly.

15

Nick changed into a full Santa suit of the highest quality, then led me out of the back of the house.

I saw a separate outbuilding ahead of us. Inside was the most amazing sleigh I had ever seen.

"It's not the Christmas Eve sleigh, that one's much bigger of course. This is more the ceremonial sleigh. There would be a riot if I turned up to an event in the 4x4," Nick said with an easy smile.

Four reindeer were already secured in front of the vehicle and they began to whinny their excitement when they saw Nick.

A young elf was in the back corner of the outbuilding chopping carrots and cabbage. He waved lazily across at us.

"We're all set, Tonks?"

"You're good to go. Hope it goes well," the elf replied, his attention already back on the vegetables.

Nick offered his hand and I accepted, then climbed into the sleigh. Nick joined me and to my delight I realised that the space was pretty tight. We were sat close to each other and my heart hammered in my chest.

"Do you always judge this competition?" I asked in the hope that regular conversation would ease my nerves.

"Oh, no. This event is my mother's thing. But the interest in it has been dwindling. People seem to be less and less interested in these old traditions. We changed the prize this year to lunch at Claus Cottage with mum and I. Normally we'd offer a pretty grand prize, but this year we just couldn't see that it made sense so we changed things up and mum asked me to judge with her too."

"Did it have an effect on anything?"

"Not really. We didn't do it for that reason. We have a budget for these things, like any other community would. The bigger budgets need to be directed towards the bigger events – the Christmas Lights Switch on, the Mince Pie Half-Marathon, even the Candy Cane Cross Country Skiing."

I shook my head. "All of those things really happen here?"

"Of course! You've missed all of the others, I'm afraid. There's the New Year's Eve Ball, too."

"Wow," I breathed. A ball in this magical setting sounded incredible.

"Yeah, the Ball's pretty nice. Although my mum is mortified that yet again I don't have a date for it."

I side-eyed him, held my breath, hoped that an invitation might follow.

"How's mum holding up?" Nick asked.

I tried to hide my disappointment. His mum was under investigation for murder! His only interest in me was needing me to prove her innocence.

"Well, she's confirmed that the mince pie was definitely one of hers. Unfortunately, she admitted that in front of Cyril and Clive."

Nick let out a low whistle. "She's got such a good heart. She can be too open and honest for her own good sometimes."

"I saw that Persephone had made a note to herself about a wedding. Do you know if she was in a relationship at all?"

"I really couldn't say. I barely knew her."

"Well I visited Dr Lancaster this morning and he couldn't tell me anything helpful really. He did find her body, but it's not like he saw anything suspicious. He couldn't say where the mince pie came from."

"That's a shame. If we knew who gave that mince pie to Persephone, we might really be on to something."

"That was my thought process too," I said, and smiled at her as we dashed through the snow.

One of the reindeer whinnied in front of us and the others copied. They seemed in their element pulling the sleigh.

"It feels like we're getting somewhere. Or, should I say, you are."

"Really?" I asked. I didn't feel that way.

"Definitely. We know the mince pie was one of mum's. That means that we know the poison wasn't added during baking."

"And I think we know that none of her other pies had poison in," I added.

"Yes! So someone's added poison just to one pie. How could someone do that?"

"I don't know," I said.

"Dip the pie in something?" Nick suggested.

"Or dip something in the pie," I said.

"That's what I said, isn't it?"

"No, they're different. I think you're right, we're getting somewhere."

Nick sighed as the sleigh slowed and stopped. We were in Santa Square and a huge stage had been erected with rows of plastic folding chairs for the audience. There was quite a turn out, I saw.

"Are you okay?" I asked.

"I'm fine. You must think I'm awful not to drop everything to help my mum. We're just making progress and now I have to stop because duty calls," he said.

"Don't worry, I'm going to get to the bottom of this," I said with a confidence I didn't actually feel.

"I know you'll do all you can, and that's plenty good enough for us. We're just so grateful that you'd stick around and try to help. I don't know how we could ever repay you."

A ticket to the New Year's Eve Ball as his date sounded a good start, I thought.

"Hey, did you make your Santa list yet?" Nick asked. He reached into his pocket and pulled out a tiny notebook and pencil, both marked with an intricate crest featuring a reindeer-pulled sleigh flying through the sky. He handed the paper and pencil to me.

"This is the Claus Crest?"

"The one and only," he confirmed.

"It's beautiful," I said.

"Thanks. Now write your list," he said with a laugh.

I closed my eyes for a moment, then wrote down what my heart most desired. It had been years since I'd asked Santa for anything, but now that I thought about it, he'd never let me down before.

16

S anta Square erupted into cheer as Nick took the stage. He'd found a stool for me and placed it off to the side, so that I could watch him and see the crowd's reaction.

The Ice Sculpture Competition was a bigger event than I had expected, and I could only imagine the expense of it all.

It was strange imagining the Claus family having to make financial decisions in among their festivities.

Nick welcomed the audience, and they clapped uproariously as if they too were proud of themselves for turning up.

"Now, we are here today as a saddened community. We are all grieving for our friend, Persephone Hyde-Barker."

A murmur of respect passed through the crowd.

"Initially, I expected that this event would be cancelled. It seemed insensitive to gather and celebrate after such a tragic, tragic incident. The Hyde-Barker family insisted that we should continue, and so we are here today in Persephone's honour."

I felt myself choke up and I barely knew the woman. Plus I hadn't warmed to the little I knew of her.

"We'll begin by paying our respects to Persephone through her art. Please give your warmest round of applause for her ice creation, which she gave a working title of Our Hero."

There were several large shapes on the stage, each covered by a cloth, and two elves in green and red costumes approached the first mass and pulled the cloth away.

The audience gave a collective gasp as Persephone's ice sculpture was revealed.

It was Santa. Not young, dimpled Nick, but the Santa from my childhood – complete with impressive beard, a round stomach and big, heavy boots.

Nick caught my eye and mouthed, "it's my dad".

A tingle ran through my body. His father was the Father Christmas of my childhood. Nick was Santa. This was all real. I really was in a winter wonderland surrounded by elves and ice sculptures and... a murderer.

I blinked and forced myself to pay attention.

The crowd continued to applaud Persephone's ice sculpture. A few people wiped their eyes with handkerchiefs in festive designs.

Right at the back of the audience, I saw a few people standing and watching. I smiled. The turnout was better than expected if there were no seats left for them.

"I'd like to invite Moira Hyde-Barker on to the stage to say a few words," Nick said.

Persephone's mother joined him on stage. Her face was ghastly white and her hands trembled.

"Thank you, Nick. Thank you everyone for being here today. It was important to me that today went ahead. Persephone was a young woman who threw herself into everything she did. She knew how hard the other entrants worked and wouldn't want that to go to waste."

There was a spattering of applause.

I noticed Dr Lancaster among the group standing at the back. He shifted awkwardly on his feet. He'd said he had been an outsider, not even a fan of Christmas.

"Persephone was a wonderful daughter. She was a valued employee. And she was a lover of all things Christmas. She would want us to celebrate in her honour. In her memory. Today, let's do exactly that."

And with those words, Moira Hyde-Barker's emotions overcame her and she left the stage in tears. I watched her go, saw a friend or relative scoop her into a hug and lead her back to the front row, where several people reached across and shook her hand.

Nick cleared his throat. The audience's attention returned to him.

"We have three finalists this year, and we'll reveal them in turn. We'll then take a quick break for voting and spiced cider," Nick explained.

The sculptures were revealed one by one.

Amorette Taylor's was a fairly simplistic snowman. I felt guilty for judging her ice sculpting abilities so harshly as soon as Nick revealed that she was ten years old. I clapped with extra enthusiasm for her.

Marz Forrest's was a gingerbread man with a fairly intricate icing pattern.

Ginger Rumples' sculpture was the last to be shown, and I could barely believe my eyes when I saw it. Her sculpture was a snow globe, with a miniature version of Candy Cane Hollow inside the globe. It was breath taking. She'd even somehow created the effect of what looked like snow falling.

I looked between her sculpture and Persephone's. There was no competition. Ginger was the obvious winner. Having heard how competitive Persephone was, maybe she would be grateful she was killed before losing.

"Three worthy contestants. Please go to the voting station, treat yourself to a warm cup of spiced cider, and be back in your seats in fifteen minutes," Nick asked.

The audience rose and filed from their seats in an orderly way that suggested the folks of Candy Cane Hollow were used to filing in and out of large events.

I watched as Ginger approached Nick, close enough that I could overhear her words.

"I can't believe you're going ahead with this!"

"Ginger, calm down. It was the Hyde-Barker family's wish," Nick said with a shrug. He glanced across at me and his eyes apologised. The thought that maybe he wanted to be back in my company as much as I wanted to be in his made my stomach flip.

He wants to be with you so you can get back to clearing his mother's name, nothing else, a voice came inside my head.

"It's completely inappropriate. What do I do when I win? I can hardly act pleased about it. I'll have to turn my acceptance speech into some eulogy for Persephone. It's rotten," Ginger crossed her arms and glared at nothing in particular.

"When you win?" Nick's dimple was revealed as he smiled at her.

"We both know I'm going to. I win every year. This is my thing, Santa. And we both know that being gracious and tactful isn't my strength," Ginger said with an eye roll.

"I can agree with that," Nick said.

"I live and breathe ice. The competition's mine. It's cute that other people even bother to enter," Ginger winked.

"You deserve to win. This snow globe you've made? I don't even understand how you can ice a sculpture inside an ice sculpture."

"Thanks, Nick. Guess I'll be coming for dinner at Claus Cottage as my prize!"

Nick laughed. "Let's see what the votes say."

"Ask Gilbert to prepare my favourite!" Ginger called.

Nick shook his head and walked back across towards me.

"You remember Ginger?" Nick asked, although she'd retreated off the stage and was dashing to beat the queue at the spiced cider stand.

"I get the impression you meet her once and never forget her," I said. He was clearly fond of her and I didn't want to offend him.

He grinned at me. "That's a pretty fair assessment! Although she's nowhere near as intense about anything else as she is about ice sculpting."

"You two have quite the history?" I tried to keep my voice nonchalant.

He raised an eyebrow. "She's like an annoying kid sister. Always hanging around, especially when I'd much rather be focusing on something – or someone – else."

I shuddered. "She's desperate to win this thing every year."

"I wouldn't phrase it that way. Let's just say that nobody has ever come close to her ice sculpting prowess."

"Persephone came close," I looked at her sculpture as I spoke. Sure, it wasn't in the same league as a whole town handcrafted inside a snow globe, but it was an impressive sculpture.

"Absolutely. And that's her first attempt, remember. Ginger's devoted her whole life to developing her skill."

"Was Ginger a little rumpled by Persephone stepping on her turf?" I asked.

Nick snickered until a tiny young elf appeared by his side with a steaming cup of spiced cider in each hand.

"For you and the lady friend," the elf said in an impossibly deep voice.

"Alright Sneck, that's very kind of you," Nick said. He accepted one drink and I took the other and said thanks.

I took a sip. The taste was rich and appley with a hint of cloves and ginger. I murmured my approval.

"Good, huh?"

"It's delicious. Everything I eat and drink here is. I don't understand how anyone could live here and not gain weight."

"Yeah, my dad had that issue," Nick said with a wink.

"Why were you laughing just then? When I asked if Ginger was..."

"Rumpled! You asked if Ginger was rumpled. Get it? Her name is Ginger Rumples," he laughed. Tiny creases appeared at the corners of his eyes. I could get used to them.

"Oh! Ha, I made a joke."

"But to answer your question, I have no idea. Ginger wouldn't show it even if she was feeling under pressure. And let me say, her sculptures are always fantastic, but this one? It's a whole other level. So maybe the competition was good for her."

"Or maybe it's a sign that she was feeling the pressure," I considered.

"You don't seriously think Ginger's the killer, surely?"

"I think it's a possibility we have to consider. Persephone was the biggest threat to her winning record."

"How can we be sure that the mince pie was even poisoned? Maybe Persephone had an allergic reaction?"

"To a mince pie?" I asked.

He shrugged. "I guess it just hit me that whoever the killer turns out to be, it's going to be a real blow to us all. Someone among us... this is really bad. And I thought I was doing an okay job taking over. What must my dad think of me?"

"Hey, you can't blame yourself. The only person who should be feeling guilty right now is the murderer, whoever he or she is."

"You're right. Wow, I don't know what we'd do without you Holly."

Sneck appeared again and cleared his throat. "Santa, the votes are in."

Sneck handed an envelope to Nick, who gave me one last smile, drained the last of his cider, and returned to the centre of the stage.

The applause was a little less restrained and the tone a little less respectful. There was some banging of feet on the floor and a few random jeers.

It seemed the good folk of Candy Cane Hollow got squiffy pretty quick. Either that or the spiced cider was stronger than I expected.

"The votes have been counted and I am delighted to announce the winner of our annual Ice Sculpture Competition! Please join me on stage and accept your applause, Ginger Rumples!"

The crowd went wild and Ginger practically cartwheeled across the stage.

She reached Nick's side and beamed from ear to ear, then addressed the audience. "I'm so honoured to be your winner, again!"

I cringed. Could she not have at least tried not to gloat, or started her acceptance with a nod of respect for Persephone?

"Well, let's give a round of applause to this year's winner, to all of our contestants, and let's raise the roof in Perse-phone Hyde-Barker's honour!" Nick interrupted. His opinion of her tactless acceptance speech cleared mirrored my own.

The audience whooped and hollered, but after a second or two it was clear that interspersed with the cheers were some boos. Some heckling.

I stiffened a little in my seat as I wondered if we were in any danger. There was still a murderer on the loose after all, and those enormous ice sculptures were ready-made murder weapons if they were pushed in the right direction.

Nick's grin was fixed in place and he clapped to a sporadic beat. It didn't seem that he'd heard the commotion.

I searched the crowd and saw a number of elves, disguised in black trousers and hoodies but with the distinctive pointed footwear that identified them. They were stomping those decorative feet in a co-ordinated rhythm, hissing and booing, and they held placards.

"Nick," I called. I got up from my seat and went to his side, then became aware that that was a strange thing to do, so gave an awkward wave.

"Hey you," he said.

"Trouble over at two o'clock," I murmured.

"Trouble at two o'clock? You're predicting trouble?"

"No, over at two o'clock. Look that way," I said. The trouble-makers weren't advancing, thankfully, but more and more of the audience had begun to notice them.

"I've got no idea what that means, but have you seen the protesters?"

"Yes! That's exactly... never mind. You've already seen them?"

"Elves in hoodies? They're hardly being discrete about it."

"And you're just ignoring them?"

"I think that's the best idea. They need to get it out of their system," Nick said. He continued to clap and grin.

I squinted my eyes and tried to make out the writing on the placards. I guessed it was their first protest since most of them were indecipherable. I could only read one and that was enough.

In beautiful hand lettering and decorated with a festive and cheerful design, the placard read:

SEND MRS CLAUS TO CANDY CANE CUSTODY

17

"How was it?" Mrs Claus asked as Nick and I let ourselves into Claus Cottage.

The ride back had been a quiet one, with Nick seeming thoughtful and pensive. I'd taken the opportunity to admire the scenery. The blanket of snow grew ever deeper but the streets were filled with people still.

The residents of Candy Cane Hollow were clearly better adjusted to winter conditions than the rest of the country. Most train routes in England ground to a halt as soon as there was so much as a leaf on the tracks, never mind a barrage of snow!

"It was fine. Ginger won, of course, and started making a tactless speech. I had to interrupt her but I don't think she noticed," Nick said.

I watched him carefully, wondering whether he was going to tell his mum about the elves protesting for her imprisonment.

"Ginger has thick skin. I'm sure if she did notice, she understood why you had to do it. Did you enjoy it, Holly?" Mrs Claus said with a smile.

"Oh! Yes! I've never seen anything quite like it before," I admitted.

"You really have arrived at the best time of the year," Mrs Claus said.

I wasn't sure what Candy Cane Hollow must be like the rest of the year. Did the inhabitants get the January blues like the rest of the world? Did they make resolutions, take part in egg hunts at Easter, escape for a bit of sun in the summer? Or was this place a winter wonderland all year around? The thoughts were pointless. I'd have to return to my house soon enough, where there wasn't so much as a piece of tinsel up.

I shook my head. I needed to focus on clearing Mrs Claus' name. Then I could move on to sorting out the rest of my life.

"Mrs Claus, we have to consider who the killer might be," I said.

Mrs Claus padded into the den and I saw that she was in the middle of polishing the Christmas tree decorations. She had a low stool set out and she sat down and continued on with the task.

I met Nick's gaze and cocked my head.

"She thinks best when her hands are busy," he said with a knowing grin.

Sure enough, Mrs Claus murmured as she polished the life out of a gold reindeer ornament.

"I've been thinking about this a lot, and I just can't believe anyone here in Candy Cane Hollow would do such a thing," she said, finally.

"I know it's hard to believe, but someone has done it. And Nick says there aren't any hotels here, so it must be a local, right?"

"I know. It's just so hard to imagine one of our own behaving like that."

"Maybe if we could get to the bottom of Persephone's notes that I found?"

"What notes were they, dear?"

"Not much. The police had already taken her computer when I got to the surgery. But her diary was still tucked into a drawer. There wasn't much of interest in there, but it did talk about a wedding."

"That's odd. Persephone was single," Mrs Claus said.

"You're sure?"

"Oh, yes. She was a very competitive person. If she'd been courting, I think the whole of Candy Cane Hollow would have heard about it."

"You think it would even have reached its way up to Claus Cottage?" I asked.

It was clear to me that the Claus family were revered like royalty. Surely, they couldn't keep up to date with all of the village's gossip.

"I wasn't close to Persephone but my mother was," Nick said.

"I wouldn't say close exactly. I knew her, of course I did, and we spent some time together. As Mrs Claus, I'm the more public face of Christmas in some ways. Nick's father was always busy at Santa HQ, just as Nick is now. I've always tried to keep involved with the community, turn up to the events, volunteer for things."

"And you're confident you'd have known if she was engaged?"

"Very. In fact, her mother spoke to me about her a few times. We were paired up a few times for Blitzen Bingo, believe it or not! Now that was fun. Her mother was concerned that she was too head-strong, and it was affecting her meeting a man."

"Interesting. Did Moira ever talk to Persephone about it?"

"Oh, yes. They bickered about it. Apparently, Persephone said she was holding out for the right man and even gave Moira the impression she'd decided who it would be. Moira was of the opinion that the whole thing was a fantasy."

"Wow," I said.

"Yes, it was very sad really. If Persephone had found someone to settle down with, she'd have been showing him off everywhere."

"Unless she couldn't," I murmured.

"Hmm?"

"What if discretion was required? Could Persephone have been involved with a married man?"

Mrs Claus gasped and the reindeer ornament jumped out of her hand. In an impressively sprightly move for an older woman, she bolted after it and let out a long breath when she caught it just before it reached the floor.

"Goodness me. Holly, are you suggesting an affair?"

"It's a possibility, surely? Persephone's potentially planning – or dreaming about – a wedding, but not talking to anyone about it."

"That kind of thing doesn't happen here," Mrs Claus said.

I laughed.

"No, she's right. We don't see much of those situations – affairs, divorces. It's not as if they're illegal or anything, but it just doesn't seem to happen."

"Neither does murder, except it has now," I reminded them.

"That's a very good point," Nick accepted.

"It isn't what's happened here, though, Holly. Persephone wouldn't have accepted that arrangement."

"Unless she saw it as a competition?"

"No," Mrs Claus said, and she shook her head.

"And it couldn't have been a man who had some other reservation about going public? Not someone newly divorced? You've already said divorces aren't common. A widower with grieving children, perhaps?"

Nick considered the question. "I can't think of anybody at all."

"There hasn't been a divorce here in almost ten years. And eligible widowers? There aren't any."

"Could it have been a woman?" I asked.

Mrs Claus blinked at me as she returned the reindeer and reached for the next ornament – a silver pinecone.

"What if Persephone was in love with another woman? Could she have felt the need to keep that secret?"

"Why on Earth would she do that?" Mrs Claus asked.

"Well, some people aren't that open-minded..."

Mrs Claus let out a harrumph. "In Candy Cane Hollow, love is love. Nobody would pull a cracker about a thing like that."

I glanced at Nick. He nodded his agreement. More and more, my desire to return to my cold house was disappearing.

"I'd guess that if Persephone had one preference, it was for the male variety, though," Mrs Claus said.

"What makes you say that?"

"Oh, she had the biggest crush on Nick! You should have seen the way she'd colour up when he was anywhere near!"

"Mother..." Nick groaned.

I laughed. I could hardly blame Persephone for finding Nick attractive.

I was about to say something light-hearted when the doorbell rang.

18

Chief Superintendent Wiggles was short, round and hairy. His eyebrows seemed to trail so far that they almost connected with his impressive sideburns, which joined the beard that didn't quite reach far enough to cover his stomach.

Nick had answered the door and led the man into the den, introducing him for my benefit.

"An outsider?" Wiggles asked with suspicion.

"Mrs Claus rescued me. My car skidded into a snowbank. I'd have died from frostbite if she hadn't found me," I blurted out.

"I see. You'll remain here until you're granted permission to leave," Wiggles said.

"Walter, please. The girl has a home to get to. It's almost Christmas," Mrs Claus pleaded with him.

"It's Chief Superintendent Wiggles while I'm on duty, please, Mrs Claus. And I'm well aware of what day it is. I'm also aware that we have a murder on our hands and nobody should leave Candy Cane Hollow."

"I thought I was the prime suspect?" Mrs Claus asked.

"You are. But I'm prepared to consider other possibilities if they present themselves, and an outsider turning up just in time for Persephone to be killed is awful convenient."

"What! I'd spent five minutes in her company before she was killed!"

"That's enough for some people," Wiggles said.

"What can we help you with, Chief Superintendent?" Nick asked.

"I've come to take Mrs Claus in for questioning," he said.

"Oh, Walter, you could have just phoned and I'd have come straight over. Could have saved you the journey," Mrs Claus said.

"That's not a problem. Shall we be going?"

"Holly's going to come with me. She'll act as my legal representative," Mrs Claus winked at me.

"Is that so?" Wiggles asked.

I felt my cheeks flush, but nodded.

"Why don't you speak to me here? It's nice and warm, and I could rustle up some hot cocoa for us all," Mrs Claus offered.

"We'll go to the station," Wiggles insisted.

I pulled my shoes back on and Mrs Claus went in search of Gilbert so she could give him instructions for the evening meal. She then realised she should try the toilet before we left, so went off again.

I stood in the entrance hall in an awkward silence with Wiggles and Nick. It seemed the only thing we could talk about was the only thing we couldn't talk about. Wiggles wouldn't discuss the case with us and we didn't want to discuss anything else.

"Ready!" Mrs Claus appeared in front of us with a biscuit tin in her hand. She held it out for Wiggles, who raised his bushy eyebrows and cleared his throat.

"I can't accept that," he said.

"Oh, what a load of turkey! Of course you can! It's only cookies, Walter! You've been eating my cookies since you were a boy," Mrs Claus said with a warm smile.

Wiggles looked to his left and right, as if scared that we might be recording the whole thing, then reached out for the biscuit tin and stuffed it into his briefcase.

"Very kind. Now we really must be leaving," he said.

He drove an old Fiat that wasn't big enough for him never mind passengers too. Mrs Claus and I crammed ourselves into the back seat while Wiggles apologised for the mess. Some people, I knew, apologised for the mess only to make you notice how tidy a place was. Wiggles was not that kind of person. His backseat was littered with sweet wrappers, old newspapers, three ties and a Christmas card for a dear friend, still in the cellophane.

"We'll take the back roads," he said.

"Thank you, dear. I always love the scenery out there," Mrs Claus said.

He swung a left away from the village itself and we were suddenly driving through a blanket of snow with open fields on both sides. I realised that he was protecting Mrs Claus from prying eyes, not treating her to the scenic route.

We arrived at Candy Cane Custody, which gave me a fright until Mrs Claus explained that the police station was inside as well as the jail. It was a squat building and much less attractive than the rest of the village, which might explain why it was set away from the shops and houses.

The inside was a pleasant surprise. The entrance lobby featured a large tastefully decorated Christmas tree, and Christmas carols piped out of the speaker in the corner.

Wiggles buzzed us through the door and lead us to an interview room. It was spacious, featuring two settees and a coffee table and an open fire that burned healthily. It didn't match up with my idea of interview rooms from all of those reality TV shows I'd watched, and I wondered if this was all to create a false sense of security.

"Drink?" Wiggles offered.

"Hot cocoa, please, dear," Mrs Claus said. She settled herself on one settee and I slid in next to her.

"Holly?"

"I'll have the same, thanks," I said.

"Any special requirements?"

"A little ground nutmeg for me, please," Mrs Claus asked.

Wiggles nodded as if he was a barista, not a Chief Superintendent about to interview his prime suspect for a murder.

"Sure, I'll have the same," I agreed.

He got up and left the room and was gone long enough that I realised he was personally making the drinks for us, and they weren't coming from a vending machine. I imagined Wiggles standing over a hot pan of milk, preparing the perfect cocoas for us.

He returned with a drink for each of us, each one in a beautiful festive mug, and started the tape recorder. We all said our names for the benefit of the tape – that bit was just as I'd seen on TV and I felt a little giddy with excitement until I reminded myself that this was real life. Mrs Claus' reputation and liberty were on the line.

"Mrs Claus, you're accused of murdering Persephone Hyde-Barker. What do you have to say about that?"

"I didn't do it," Mrs Claus said.

"Is that all you have to say?"

"What else do you want to know, dear?" Mrs Claus asked.

"Where were you at the time of her death?" Wiggles asked.

"Well, I was at Claus Cottage with witnesses – my son Nick, and Holly here. But that doesn't really help you, Chief Superintendent."

"What do you mean?" Wiggles took a sip of his cocoa and sat back on the other settee.

"The time of her death wasn't the time of her murder, was it? She'd eaten some of the mince pie and I imagine poisons and things take time to work their magic. Not magic. That was an unfortunate choice of word."

"It certainly was. Is that how you consider all this? A little bit of magic?"

"Of course not. It's a tragedy. I cannot believe that this has happened on my watch," Mrs Claus said.

"On my watch, not yours. I'm the Chief Superintendent."

"And I'm Mrs Claus," she said.

Wiggles swallowed.

"Anyway. You accept that the mince pie was one of yours?"

"I believe so, yes," Mrs Claus said and shook her head regretfully.

"And we know that the poison was inside the mince pie. That means that either your ingredients were tampered with, or you killed her."

"There are other options," I interrupted.

"Like what?"

"Like someone interfering with the mince pie after it was baked, in order to frame Mrs Claus," I suggested.

Mrs Claus gasped by my side. "Who would want to do such a thing?"

"I don't know," I admitted.

"I'm not sure how someone would interfere with a mince pie, anyway. It sounds like a fanciful idea," Wiggles said.

"But there must be other evidence. Why on Earth would Mrs Claus use her own mince pie to poison someone? That leads you straight to her as the prime suspect!"

"Criminals often aren't very clever. No offence, Mrs Claus," Wiggles said.

"None taken. He's got a point, dear."

"For acts of passion, yes. Unplanned murders where someone snaps. But this was planned. No other mince pies have been poisoned, which tells us that Persephone was targeted for some reason. You should be looking for people with some kind of grudge against her," I suggested.

Wiggles leaned in. "Do you have any suggestions? I'm a fair officer, I'll explore all avenues. But you do know that we need this wrapped up like a present before Christmas?"

"What?" I asked.

"We can't have a murder case distracting everyone from the business of the season. Presents need to be delivered, the magic of Christmas has to be everyone's priority."

"So, you're suggesting that you lock Mrs Claus up for a crime she hasn't committed?"

"Lock her up?" Wiggles asked.

"Lock me up?" Mrs Claus asked.

"In Candy Cane Custody!" I exclaimed.

Wiggles gave an uproarious laugh and almost allowed his cocoa to spill over the sides of his mug.

"We don't lock people up! What do you think we are, animals?"

"But I thought..."

Wiggles rose from his chair, still laughing, and left the room again. He returned a moment later with a glossy catalogue.

CANDY CANE CUSTODY WELCOME PACK, it read.

I flicked through the catalogue and saw neat little en-suite rooms, each with a large window overlooking the snow-covered fields behind the building. On the next page, photographs of the state-of-the-art gymnasium and swimming pool. Further through, a sample meal plan that made my stomach grumble. It went on and on.

"Candy Cane Custody's a hotel?" I asked, confused.

"No, dear, we don't have hotels here. Candy Cane Custody is jail."

"And if Mrs Claus killed Persephone, she'll live the rest of her days in there," Wiggles said.

I had to admit that didn't sound terrible, but of course it would be the loss of her reputation and freedom that would be worst for her.

"Now, if we can get back to the questions. Mrs Claus, why did you kill Persephone Hyde-Barker?"

"I didn't!" Mrs Claus exclaimed.

"Did you kill her for money?"

"What?"

"Did you kill her for revenge?"

I leaned forward and saw that Wiggles was reading a template list of questions.

"Look, she didn't kill her, so you can put those questions away. Let's use this time to see if we can help each other out."

"I do not accept bribes," Wiggles said, for the benefit of the tape. He even looked at the tape as he said the words, probably so there could be no possibility that his reply would be muffled or unclear.

"Have you found anything from her computer yet?" I asked.

"We haven't taken her computer," Wiggles said.

I rolled my eyes. "Not Mrs Claus. I mean Persephone."

"I know. We haven't taken her computer," he repeated.

"You did, I went to visit Dr Lancaster and pay my respects and the computer from reception was gone."

Wiggles shrugged. "We didn't take it."

"Well, who did? Don't you think it's curious?" I asked.

"Not really. She wasn't going to need it, was she? I'd guess that Dr Lancaster cleared it away. It's a good chance to update things, I guess."

"Or maybe the killer returned and stole it to get rid of some incriminating evidence!" Mrs Claus said.

"That would be dumb. Do you know how much Candy Cane Television there is on the High Street?"

"Candy Cane Television?" I asked.

"CCTV," Wiggles said.

"There's – hold on – there's CCTV? Have you watched it?"

"You think I've got time for that?" Wiggles asked.

I blinked. He had time to hand prepare hot cocoas with ground nutmeg but no time to review CCTV evidence.

"I'll do it," I offered.

"Oh, I don't..."

"I have nothing but time on my hands. Let me be useful, please," I asked.

Wiggles shrugged. "Well, fine. I'll have the boys request it and I'll let you know when it's here."

"Thank you. Is there anything else we should know about? Like the CCTV. Anything you're perhaps too busy to do? Maybe I could help with other things too," I said.

"There is something. I've got a pile of paperwork so high it's nearly as tall as me. If you're really so bored, you can have a party filing it all away!"

"Oh, erm..." I spluttered.

"I'm kidding! Nobody's bored enough to want that job. Now, it doesn't seem like we've got far today. Mrs Claus, you want to use this chance to confess? Get anything off your chest? It looks good if you co-operate – you're looking at a bigger room, an en-suite with a bath not just a shower, maybe even a better view. They're not benefits to be sniffed at."

"I simply can't help you, dear. You know I would if I could."

"How long until the CCTV will be ready?" I asked.

"Only a few hours. You really are keen for work, aren't you?" Wiggles joked.

"I'm keen for the killer to be caught," I corrected him and the smile slid off his face.

"Wiggles, how's your aunt Dolores?" Mrs Claus asked.

"She's doing very well, thank you. Now, I think we're done here. I'll organise a ride home for you ladies," Wiggles said.

"That's most kind," Mrs Claus said.

Wiggles stopped the tape recording and left the room.

I looked across at Mrs Claus. "Are you okay?"

"Fine, dear. It's always nice to catch up with a friend. Walter's too busy to chat a lot of the time, with all of his responsibilities here. Such a big family he has, too!"

"The Wiggles family," I murmured with a smile.

"Oh, no, not Wiggles. The family name is Smythe. Walter thought it was hard to appear independent while sharing the same name as so many local folk, so he changed his surname."

"And he chose Wiggles?"

"It was an old nickname. He's been Wiggles for as long as I've known him. People used to say he wiggled when he walked."

"This place really is unique," I said.

"Is it growing on you, dear?"

I considered the question. I pictured how the folks of Candy Cane Hollow all took the time to wave at each car that drove by, and how Mrs Claus had prepared food and drink even for the police officers investigating her.

"It really is. I'm not sure how homely home will feel after this," I admitted.

"Oh, Holly, anywhere can feel like home. All it takes is a few little touches. I believe that your home should be your own wonderland. A place where you can kick off your shoes and feel safe and at peace."

"That sounds wonderful," I said.

"It is. But you're still young. You're out in the world I bet, going from party to party. Dating young men, I imagine! Fancy dinners and long work lunches. Maybe a peaceful home is more of an old woman's thing."

I smiled at the vision of my life that Mrs Claus had imagined. It was so far from the truth. A home that felt like a sanctuary sounded like just what I wanted.

19

W ith a few hours to spare until the CCTV was ready to view, I decided to join Nick over at Santa HQ.

"Busy day?" I asked.

"It is, yeah," he said.

"You seem distracted. What's on your mind?"

"Other than my mum being hauled into the clink as a murder suspect? I'm worried that Wiggles will be feeling under pressure to get this case tied up before Christmas Eve. You know he's made this place a no-fly zone? Nobody can enter or leave. Which makes sense. But if that includes me, we have real issues when we get to December 24th," Nick said with a sigh.

"You mean you might not be able to deliver the presents?" I asked. I could barely believe that I was saying those words with sincerity, but I was past the point of being my normal cynical self. Nick was Santa, and Persephone's murder was placing Christmas at risk.

If I hadn't felt under pressure to clear Mrs Claus' name before, I really did as that realisation sank in.

"I just don't know. I have no idea what protocol should be in this kind of a situation, and I don't think Wiggles knows either."

"He seems fair," I murmured.

"He is. But he's going to need to close this case, and if he can't find a better suspect than my mum, she's going to end up taking the blame."

I swallowed. I was surprised to find that tears filled my eyes. I already felt so attached to Mrs Claus.

"Anyway. Let's talk about something else. Tell me more about you, Holly. When you're not driving into snowbanks, what do you normally like to do?"

It sounded like such a first date question that I visibly cringed. Nick was a friend in need of distraction, that was all.

"Well, I was driving home after my last day at a locum GP contract. So, I'm officially unemployed."

"That's good or bad?"

I laughed. "It will become bad at some point, but for now I have a bit of money to get me by for a month or two and I quite fancy a break from all of that hustle and bustle."

"What do you want to do next?"

I considered the question. "I don't know. I've been working as a locum for years and I used to enjoy getting to change jobs so often. Now, I'm not sure it's what I want any more."

"Maybe an opportunity will present itself when the time is right," Nick smiled.

"I'm sure it will," I agreed, although I didn't believe it. I'd never been a person who had had opportunities just fall in my lap. Every break I'd had in life, I'd had to go out and find myself.

We arrived at Santa HQ and Mitzy was there by the main door again, clipboard in hand.

"Stuffing spillage in Zone 4. The appropriate elf has been reprimanded," she said.

"Reprimanded? Is that how we deal with mistakes?" Nick asked.

Mitzy cleared her throat. "It's happening too often. I thought a message needed to be sent."

I stifled laughter as I walked behind the two of them.

We reached Nick's office and Mitzy promised to make us hot cocoas, then left.

"She really is a character," I said.

"I'm a little scared of her," Nick admitted with a wink.

"I thought elves were all merry and bright."

"Oh, that old chestnut. Some of them are. They're just like us, each one comes with their own personality."

The phone on Nick's desk rang.

He reached for it and I realised that rather than simply being a rather ugly brown phone, it was a turkey and all the trimmings phone. The receiver that Nick had picked up was one of the turkey legs.

I let out a laugh and had to get up and walk over to his window to distract myself. A turkey phone!

Candy Cane Hollow looked busier than ever as I gazed out. The traffic was heavy by the village's standards since my arrival, and noisier than it had to be since each car beeped its horn at every person it drove by. Sometimes the cars stopped and a pedestrian would approach the window for a chat, the other cars piling up behind.

That kind of behaviour would have drove me mad back home in London, but nobody seemed to mind here. Being neighbourly seemed to be a higher priority than arriving at their destination on time.

"That was Wiggles," Nick said.

"Oh, no. What now?" I asked.

"The CCTV's ready for you and he's offered to come and pick you up in ten minutes."

"That's awful nice of him," I said.

Nick shrugged. "He has a car, you don't. Or at least, yours isn't in any fit state to drive."

"True," I said. I'd managed to put the thought of my car out of my head, but it would be another thing for me to sort at some point. It had probably been towed away, I expected. I'd have to pay to get it back, just for the privilege of confirming that it should be written off. Or maybe they wrote it off right away. I had no idea. I'd never been in the position before.

"Hot cocoas," Mitzy announced as she pushed the door open. She carried an ornate tray with two glasses on. Each glass held a hot cocoa that looked too beautiful to drink. She'd somehow managed to get the layered effect that the hipster coffee shops in town loved to do, and had topped our drinks with a tall mound of cream, sprinkles and an actual cherry on top.

"You've outdone yourself," Nick said with a grin.

"Thank you," I said.

Mitzy gave us a smile and then left us to it. No doubt she had to get back to her clipboard.

"I really hope the CCTV shows something," I said.

"Me too," Nick agreed.

"It could be the breakthrough we need. If someone stole Persephone's computer, that's got to be suspicious, right?"

"Unless they're just a kleptomaniac."

"You have many of these at Candy Cane Hollow?" I asked.

"None to my knowledge. But I didn't think we had any murderers either," Nick said.

"Fair point."

I drank my cocoa and picked up on the subtle cherry flavour. Hence the cherry on top. It was delicious, but I worried that all of these cocoas couldn't be good for my waistline.

After a few minutes, Mitzy returned. "Chief Superintendent Wiggles has arrived."

"Thank you," I said. I big my goodbye to Nick – promising to update him afterwards – and followed Mitzy back to the main doors.

"So, unknown female. What are your intentions with Nick?"

"What? First of all, I'm not unknown, we met yesterday. And I don't have any intentions with Nick," I said.

Mitzy narrowed her eyes. "I'll be keeping an eye on things and let me warn you, I'll report what I see to Mrs Claus if I have to!"

I could see why Nick found her intimidating. "Okay, well, I'll take that warning on board."

Wiggles sat in his tiny car, the engine still running. His mouth was moving and I wondered if he was on a call, but he spotted me and waved me in. As soon as I opened the passenger door, I realised he was singing along to Christmas songs.

"It's so good of you to come and get me," I said as I fastened my seatbelt. Mitzy watched from the door as we drove away.

"You're very welcome. Now, you know this one? Sing along," he insisted, and I quietly joined in with him to the rest of *Last Christmas*.

"What's your favourite Christmas song?" Wiggles asked, to my surprise.

My cheeks flamed. "I've always quite liked *All I Want For Christmas Is You*, I guess."

"Mariah Hairy?"

"Carey, but yes," I said.

"Good choice. It says a lot about a person, you know," he said. *Last Christmas* began to play again, and I guessed by the repetition that I didn't have to ask which festive song was his own favourite.

We reached Candy Cane Custody after just eight repetitions of his favourite Christmas song and when we reached the reception area, Dr Lancaster was there.

He jumped up from his seat in the waiting area as soon as he saw Wiggles, then eyed me with suspicion.

"Dr Lancaster, good to see you again. How can I help?"

"Any news?" The medic asked.

"Not since you rang me this morning right as I was brushing my teeth," Wiggles said, then offered a grin.

"Ah, yes, that was rude of me. I'm just so desperate to be of service, it's all I've known my whole life. I make situations better."

"Of course you do. But you can leave this one to us. Unless you think of anything that might be helpful."

Dr Lancaster shifted a little on his feet.

"Doc?"

"There is something. It's probably nothing, but it occurred to me. Probably nonsense."

"What is it?" Wiggles asked.

Dr Lancaster leaned in and lowered his voice by barely a fraction. "Persephone had handed in her notice at work."

"Now, that's not nothing at all. When did she do that?"

He shrugged. "Oh, I don't remember exactly. A few days before... before what happened."

"She give a reason?"

"She said she wouldn't have time to continue working."

"Any idea what that means?" Wiggles asked.

"Well, no."

"You didn't ask?" I asked. Dr Lancaster shot me a glance but Wiggles didn't seem to mind me asking the question.

"Persephone was my secretary. I did try to keep some boundaries," Dr Lancaster said.

"Had you started looking for her replacement?" I asked. Wiggles raised an eyebrow.

"No, I hadn't. This is arrogant of me, but I suspected that it may have been a rather rash decision. I wanted her to have the option of reconsidering. She was a good worker, and we all know how much work it is to train someone new."

"And did she give you any sign before her death that she had changed her mind?"

"She didn't."

"Other than that, she seemed fine. No worries? Nothing out of character?"

"I really couldn't say. We worked together, yes, but we were in different rooms all day long."

"You must have spoken to her, though. You must have had time to have some sort of communication with her during the working day?"

Dr Lancaster shrugged. "We emailed. She'd bring in a hot cocoa for me. I guess she did seem a little different. There must have been something she was planning. She wasn't the kind of woman who would just up and leave a secure job for no reason."

"This is interesting. You've been very, very helpful Dr

Lancaster. Please, do get in touch if you remember anything else."

"It's been helpful? You think this might help you find out..."

"It's been very helpful. Now I have an appointment to get to, and I know you'll have patients waiting."

Dr Lancaster took the hint and we left him in the reception area.

"He's been a big help, then?" I asked as Wiggles showed me to a small room near the reception desk. Although not large, the room was furnished comfortably and included a settee, a desk and a vinyl record player.

"We get them from time to time. Normally they're people with too much time on their hands, not professionals like him."

"You get who from time to time?"

"People who want to involve themselves in the case, help out as much as they can which normally translates into taking time away from the genuine avenues of investigation. But, as I say, normally it's a person who likes the attention or doesn't have anything else going on in their life."

"He seemed pretty cut up about her death when I went to pay my respects."

"Oh, certainly. He's lost a darn good secretary. It's good that he wants to help."

"Definitely," I agreed.

"You were great out there. Those questions you asked – I hadn't thought of them myself! I might bring you in on every interview I do. Hey, I'll make a drink," Wiggles said.

My stomach gurgled. "Oh, no, thank you so much but I've just had one."

Wiggles looked baffled by the suggestion of a person refusing a hot cocoa, but recovered after a second or two.

"You want to just get straight to the CCTV, then?" He asked.

"If that's okay," I said. I felt as if I'd turned up to my parents' house for dinner and then told them I'd be eating in my bedroom.

Wiggles fetched a laptop and showed me how to work my way through the video footage, how to skip ahead, go back, pause and zoom in.

I thanked him and he left me to it.

The footage was grainy and not at all helped by the fact that snow fell constantly. While the camera was across the road and did, in theory, show the whole of Dr Lancaster's surgery, the window which Persephone's desk was behind had the blinds closed.

The door, however, had no blinds and was unobstructed – other than by the fat lumps of snow falling in front of the camera.

I settled in and tried to stay focused on the CCTV.

It was a dull job, and I could see why Wiggles hadn't jumped to devote the hours to doing it.

On the day of Persephone's murder, there was movement outside the surgery as cars drove by and people walked past. An escaped reindeer even sauntered by at one point, its handler running after it a few moments later.

Dr Lancaster arrived with a briefcase under his arm. Persephone arrived shortly afterwards, her arms full carrying a large handbag and what looked like a tote lunch bag.

Patients entered and left the clinic and three of them carried wrapped up gifts that they didn't leave the surgery with. I made a note of that. The difficulty was that these people were strangers to me and I couldn't make out any

features that distinguished them. I had only recognised Dr
Lancaster and Persephone because I had met them.

I watched as Mrs Claus pulled up and we entered the
surgery together. Mrs Claus carried nothing into the surgery,
although that detail didn't matter as I knew the mince pie
was already on Persephone's desk with a bite taken out of it
when we arrived.

I continued watching, until I saw the ambulance arrive.
Persephone was carried away. The police arrived. Dr
Lancaster stood in the surgery's doorway for a long time. It
looked as though he was crying.

He closed the door at some point and remained inside
for a long time.

He left after 8pm and the police left after him. Nobody
entered or left until Dr Lancaster returned the next
morning.

I continued watching, grateful that Wiggles had told me
how to accelerate the speed so I didn't have to watch it in
real time.

There was much more footfall past the surgery on this
second day, and virtually everyone who walked by peered
into the surgery window. Word had spread quickly about
Persephone's death, that much was clear.

I watched as I walked into the surgery to pay my
respects. Patients filed in and out.

Dr Lancaster left at lunch and returned fifteen minutes
later with a brown paper bag.

More patients filed in and out.

The police returned and stayed for quite a while.

The CCTV – only produced for the day of the murder
and the day after – eventually finished and I felt no wiser.

Nobody had left with the computer. How bizarre.

There was a tap on the door and Wiggles appeared with

a hot cocoa for each of us. "Thought you might be ready for one now?"

I flashed him a grateful smile. "You're a mind reader! I'd love one, thank you."

"How are you getting on?"

"I've watched it all, and there's not much there. Except, three people took wrapped gifts into the surgery the day of Persephone's murder. I wonder if one of those gifts contained the poisoned mince pie."

"Nope," Wiggles shook his head.

"How do you know?"

"We found the presents in Dr Lancaster's room. They were all still wrapped. We opened them, to check their contents. Two of them were World's Best Doctor mugs, and the other was a World's Best Doctor box of chocolates."

"Wow," I said. I wondered how many of those chintzy gifts he received every year. As a locum, I'd never been in one place long enough to receive gifts from patients.

"Great, huh!"

"And we have no way of telling whether any person who entered the surgery had a mince pie for Persephone?"

"Not really. It could have been taken in inside anyone's bag. Even in a coat pocket. The thing that strikes me as odd, though, is why anyone would take a mince pie in just for her, not Dr Lancaster too."

"Well, they didn't want to poison him," I said.

"Sure, but they just needed to make sure that she got the poisoned one. To leave Dr Lancaster out completely? That's not the way folks do things in Candy Cane Hollow."

"But you just said that Dr Lancaster had those gifts arriving? Those people hadn't brought a separate gift for Persephone," I said.

Wiggles laughed. "Oh, Persephone liked cash! She had a

tub on her desk for people to drop a few coins in rather than buy her a gift. Apparently, she was saving up for something."

"That's interesting. I didn't see the tub on her desk," I said.

"We took it. We wanted to check all of the coins for traces of poison. If we'd found any, we'd know it was someone who'd gone into the surgery that day."

"And was there any?"

"Nope," Wiggles said.

I sighed. "So basically it could have been someone who was there that day and just too smart to contaminate their coins with poison. Or someone who was there that day but too tight to give cash. Or it might be someone who wasn't there that day."

"That's exactly it," Wiggles said.

"Well, I think I've got everything I can from today. Thank you for letting me do this."

"Oh, it's an honour! I don't get many bigwigs from the city wanting to come in and look through things."

I grimaced as I remembered the false pretences I'd allowed Wiggles to believe.

"I need to tell you, I'm not a city bigwig. I'm unemployed, I live on my own, I..."

"Holly, none of that stuff matters. It's clear to me that Mrs Claus thinks the world of you. That makes you a bigwig in my book."

20

I decided to decline Wiggles' kind offer of another lift in the tiny Fiat, and head back on foot.

The CCTV hadn't been helpful. Wiggles had been right. He was an experienced police officer and I should have trusted that he knew where to focus his time and energy.

Maybe the very idea of me attempting to investigate was laughable.

"No," I said aloud.

A group of people walking towards me looking at me with curiosity. "Are you okay there?"

"I need to find Ginger Rumples," I blurted out.

"Well, you're heading the right way friend!" One of the group, a tall man with a grey beard, congratulated me.

"You'll find her at The Polar Arms, just off the High Street," a woman among the group told me.

"That's great, thank you," I said, stunned that discovering someone's location could be so easy. I could be the killer on my way to find my next victim!

I wondered what Ginger was doing at the pub and

hoped she hadn't drank one too many hot cocoas and gloated over her ice sculpting victory.

I trudged through the snow – very grateful for the sensible footwear that Mrs Claus had found for me – and made my way to The Polar Arms. A life-sized polar bear statue stood guard by the front door. Candy Cane Hollow sure was a place that enjoyed a good statue.

I pushed the heavy door open and felt the warmth wrap around me right away.

The pub was small and cosy, with a wooden bar that stretched the length of the place, high bar stools along it, and a neat row of booth seats by the window.

A huge Christmas tree was decorated with gold and red decorations and stood proudly right by the door. Festive fairy lights twinkled along the edge of the bar and all around the edges of the ceiling.

In the space by the door, there was an older man and woman singing Christmas songs. They seemed to have no real talent but they made up for that in enthusiasm, and several of the patrons clapped along to the music.

A brick fireplace stood at the far end of the room, logs burning away.

I felt myself shudder a little from the effects of the place.

I scanned the booth tables for Ginger, but couldn't see her. Maybe she'd already left.

I quite fancied a drink – something cold and not cocoa – so perched myself on a stool at the bar.

"Can I help you?" Ginger's voice came. I looked up and there she was, behind the bar pouring a pint.

"Ginger! You work here?"

"Ice sculpting doesn't pay the bills, even when you are the reigning champion," she said with a smile.

"Oh, I can imagine."

"Drink?" She offered, and I realised that she didn't quite know who I was.

"Sure, I'll get a sparkling water," I said.

She nodded and made the drink, slid it across the bar to me. Her attention already seemed to be moved to check out whether anyone was ready for a refill.

"We met briefly. Do you remember? I'm staying at Claus Cottage," I said.

The heads of everyone else sitting at the bar turned and looked at me, and I felt my cheeks flush.

"You're the one Mrs Claus rescued?" Ginger asked.

"That's me," I said.

She narrowed her eyes a little. "Aren't you well enough to go back home yet? You must have a million things to do before the big day."

I laughed nervously. "Well, not really. Christmas hasn't been that big of a deal for me the last few years."

The people who had just stopped looking at me returned their focus to me.

"I do love Christmas! I just, erm, I live alone and..."

"You don't have to explain to these guys. Leave it alone, you lot. Get back to your drinks," Ginger scolded them. They all did as she'd said.

"Thanks," I said.

She shrugged. "It's not a big deal. Some people just aren't as festive. I guess I'm confused about why you'd stick around at Claus Cottage if Christmas isn't your thing, though."

"Well, I, it's not..."

"Unless you've got eyes on the new Santa, of course," she said with a wink.

My cheeks flamed. I knew it. I worried that there could be a risk I might set the Christmas tree on fire with them.

Ginger burst into a fit of giggles and reached for a tray of freshly washed glasses, which she began to dry.

"I'm kidding with you."

"The two of you seem pretty close," I said.

Ginger swatted at the air. "He's like my annoying brother. Sure, the female population of Candy Cane Hollow go a little nuts for him, but I don't see the appeal. I still remember when we were kids and he managed to fit a candy cane in his mouth so tight it had to be removed under local anaesthetic!"

I allowed myself to laugh at that image, although I'd done my fair share of silly things too. As a child and as an adult.

"That's funny. You seem to be more focused on your art than anything else, anyway. What did you think to the other sculptures?"

"Oh, they were nice," she said. She was trying to be a gracious winner, but I could tell that it was an effort for her.

"Persephone's Santa was really something, huh?" I asked.

She eyed me. "Getting the conversation back to Santa, huh? Maybe you are only here for Nick's charms. You wouldn't be the first."

"What does that mean?"

"Well, Persephone's sculpture for one thing. It was fine. The nose was wrong, and there was no colouration. People don't realise that you can literally paint with the ice if you sculpt it right. That's how you can tell a professional from an amateur. But it was obvious she was going to do something that Nick would love, and I guess as a first attempt it was fine."

"She wanted to impress Nick?"

Ginger rolled her eyes. "She had a mad crush on him. It's

obvious that her sudden interest in sculpture was because of the prize."

"Dinner with him?"

"Exactly. Now, I've had more hot dinners at Claus Cottage than at my own home. It's no real prize to me. I don't compete for the prize, though. I compete to win."

"Would Persephone really be so desperate to have a meal with Nick? He seems like a pretty approachable guy."

"It's what the dinner would lead to, that's my guess. She'd been buttering Mrs Claus up all year, showing herself to be the perfect daughter-in-law. Mrs Claus really wants Nick settled down."

"A wedding," I murmured, remembering the note in Persephone's diary.

"An enormous wedding is what it would be. Santa's wife is almost more revered in Candy Cane Hollow than Santa himself."

"And you seriously didn't fancy that role for yourself?" I asked. It sounded pretty good to me.

Ginger scoffed. "It's not my style. You're welcome to him, honestly."

"I'm not interested," I said, although I didn't think my voice sounded very convincing.

Ginger raised an eyebrow and then moved down the bar to take another customer's order.

I took a sip of my water and considered what she'd said. She hadn't been worried about Persephone's entry. In fact, it sounded like she'd known what her sculpture would be before she saw it.

Sure, Ginger was blunt and a little tactless, but I liked her. She seemed like a straight talker. If she was the killer, I thought there was a chance she'd have just admitted it.

And her theory about Persephone's reasons for entering was very interesting.

I took another sip, waved my farewell to Ginger, and left The Polar Arms.

~

BACK AT CLAUS COTTAGE, I found Mrs Claus hanging out of an upstairs window with some kind of extendable pole in her hand.

"You're home! Good to see you, dear!" She exclaimed as she saw me.

"What are you doing?" I called up to her.

"Decorating the garden! I've always wanted to do this but never had time. What do you think?"

I looked across at the snow in front of the cottage and realised that she was using the pole contraption to draw a Christmas scene in it. She'd already finished a rather basic looking Christmas tree, and was working on a snowman by the side of it.

"It looks great!" I said.

Cyril and Clive ambled over and inspected her artwork too. "This is really something, Mrs C."

"Oh, stop, it's just a doodle. But it's fun! Come on up, Holly. Have a go with me."

"Okay!" I agreed. I went inside, took off my sensible winter boots, and walked upstairs.

Mrs Claus was in a guest bedroom and grinned when I entered.

"Good day, dear?"

"It's been interesting. I watched the CCTV and that really wasn't helpful, and then I saw Ginger. She has an interesting theory."

"That's nice dear. Now, hold the end like this, and you can finish Mr Frost. Give him a nice scarf, maybe?" Mrs Claus held the pole out to me.

"Mr Frost?"

"He says friends call him Jack," Mrs Claus said, then giggled at her own joke.

"Jack Frost the snowman. I like it," I said.

I laughed and took it from her, then attempted to get the other end to the right bit of snow. It was harder than it looked.

"You know all of this will be covered by more snow soon?" I asked.

"That's wonderful! That means we get to make a different picture!"

"That's a good way of looking at it. Do you want to hear what Ginger had to say?"

"Only if you want to share. I wouldn't want to pry."

"She thinks that Persephone was lining herself up to marry Nick," I said.

"Oh!" Mrs Claus gasped and covered her mouth.

"Erm... does that surprise you?" I asked.

"Goodness, dear, is that relevant?"

"It could be, yes," I said, although I hadn't worked out how yet.

"Well, yes, she really had an eye for Nick. I don't think that was a secret."

"Did she and Nick have any kind of relationship?"

Mrs Claus shook her head. "Not really. I felt for Persephone, I really did. She had such an eye for him, and he never really knew who she was. It's not Nick's fault, there are so many people here and only one Santa. They all know who he is. He does try, he really does, but he's always struggled with names."

"So they hadn't dated before or anything?"

"Nick's never dated. I wish he would. I want him to settle down with the right woman."

"Hold on. Did you suggest the change to the sculpture competition's prize as a way of setting him up with someone?"

Mrs Claus giggled a little. "Absolutely not! It never occurred to me! And I wouldn't have done it, even if I'd thought of the idea. Ginger has her strengths but she's not Nick's type. And she was always going to win."

"Even with Persephone taking part?"

"Yes, I'm afraid so. Ginger's unbeatable. You've seen her work now, she's a class act when it comes to sculptures."

"So Persephone did have a crush on Nick. And in her diary she was writing notes about weddings. Could she have had some plan to get the two of them together? Or was there someone else she was involved with?"

"I can't imagine Persephone being in a relationship and the whole of Candy Cane Hollow not knowing about it."

"But what if there was some reason it had to be secret for a while longer? I just can't get my head around it. It's there, I know it is, it's just waiting for me to put it all together."

"Speak to Nick, dear. See if he has any ideas. He'll be home for dinner," Mrs Claus said.

We continued to take it in turns drawing in the snow, until the fresh snowfall came down so fast it was erasing each line we drew straight away.

We admitted defeat and Mrs Claus went downstairs to supervise Gilbert's cooking.

I remained upstairs and looked out of the window for a while, watching the snow fall. It really was beautiful.

The grey streets of my neighbourhood would seem even

more harsh after experiencing Candy Cane Hollow. Maybe I should at least pop in and see August.

I reached for my phone and dialled her number.

She answered immediately and sounded a little out of breath.

"Did you get it?" She hissed down the phone.

"August?"

"Holly?"

"Yes, were you expecting someone else?" I said with a laugh.

"Darn it. I thought you were Tom. I'm waiting for a call. Can we speak later?"

"Sure!" I said. She'd hung up before I'd finished the word, and I sat and looked at the device. Was there some emergency?

I typed out a quick message to her asking if everything was okay.

The dots appeared immediately to let me know that she was typing a reply.

NO!!!!! DISASTER!!! JEB'S MAIN XMAS GIFT OUT OF STOCK!! TOM ON HUNT @ OTHER STORES. PRAY FOR US!!

I had to read the message to make sure that I'd understood the disaster correctly. A gift that August had decided her baby wanted wasn't available for an occasion he was too young to understand or remember? It didn't sound like a disaster to me.

But who was I to judge. August had always been a tad neurotic.

There was a rap on the door behind me and I turned to see Nick. He smiled and revealed that dimple.

"Mum said you wanted to chat to me?"

"I did? Oh, sure, I did," I said.

"Shall we walk and talk? I've had my head in wish lists at my desk all day. I need to stretch my legs a little."

"Sounds good," I said.

We got into our biggest coats and sensible boots, and wrapped up in hats and gloves. As soon as Nick opened the door, the frigid air greeted me, and the snow crunched under my feet.

I held out my hand and watched as chunky snowdrops fell on my glove.

"I've never seen snow like this," I said.

"It's really something, huh," Nick agreed.

"Oh! It's even more pretty now," I exclaimed as the streetlights came on.

"It sure is," Nick said.

We walked in a companionable silence for a few moments, each lost in our own thoughts.

"It's so quiet out," I said.

"Dinner time. We eat like clockwork here, and nobody ever wants to miss a meal," Nick explained.

"I can understand that. If I had Gilbert preparing my meals all the time I'd never want to leave the kitchen."

Nick grinned. "He's a good cook. What did you want to talk to me about?"

"I don't know, really. I was chatting to your mum earlier and she suggested I get your thoughts on things."

"Okay, sure."

"I've watched all of the CCTV from outside the surgery and it doesn't show anything conclusive. Nobody walked in with an obvious mince pie, and nobody walked out with a computer."

"That's a shame, although I guess it was always unlikely that it would be caught on video. You can't see what happens inside?"

"The blinds are drawn," I said.

"Hmm, that's odd. Every time I went by, they were open. Persephone used to wave out at me."

"She had a crush on you, apparently," I felt my own cheeks flush as I spoke, as if I was admitting my own feelings.

"Really? Nah. I don't think so," Nick said.

"Are you good at picking up on those things?" I heard the hint of flirtation in my voice and wished I could slap myself.

Nick laughed. "Okay, you got me. I'm pretty much useless in that whole department. Always have been. Having a girl as a best friend didn't help since everyone assumed I'd just marry her."

"And that's not the plan?"

"Oh, no way. Ginger and I have definitely friend zoned each other."

"She knows you well, though?"

"Better than she'd like to, probably."

"It was Ginger who told me Persephone had a crush on you," I said.

Nick's face grew serious.

"Does that change anything?" I asked.

He let out a long breath. It was visible in the air, as if he was a dragon blowing out smoke.

"I guess. I'd trust what Ginger says. If she says it, it's true," he said. He shifted on his feet, then reached down, grabbed a mound of snow, and before I knew it had tossed the snowball at me.

"Hey!" I cried, but he was already making a dash for it as best he could in the deep snow.

I ducked down and collected my own snow, patted it into a ball, and threw it at him as hard as I could. I watched in horror as it hit him right in the middle of his back and caused him to lose his balance.

He groaned as he crumpled into the snow.

I ran across to him awkwardly.

"Oh, my goodness. Have I killed you?" I shouted in panic.

I heard his laughter and felt relief flood through me. "Killed me? That was a savage attack but I think I'll survive it."

"I'm so sorry! Who knew I could throw like that?"

"Clearly not me or I wouldn't have started the snowball war. Can we call a truce?" Nick asked as he pulled himself into a sitting position. He was covered in snow and I leaned in and gently wiped it away from his face.

Nick held out a hand and I offered my own, then squealed as he pulled me down into the snow with him. He laughed and I laughed and I wondered how I'd ever manage to leave this place.

"I can't believe you did that!" I shrieked as I felt the cold spread through my trousers.

"Oh, come on. I'd have no self-respect if I didn't!"

Our eyes met and I felt a jolt of electricity run through me. We were close enough to kiss. All I'd have to do is lean in just a little, and my lips would meet his.

Nick cleared his throat and the spell was broken. "Come on, let's get you home before you freeze."

We each struggled to get up and began the short walk. Claus Cottage was visible in front of us, but it was uphill and we walked carefully so as now to fall – again.

"Wiggles said that Persephone had a little dish on her desk at work for donations, instead of Christmas gifts. I thought maybe she was saving up for something. A wedding, perhaps since that was in her diary?"

"She's always done that," Nick said.

"She has?"

"For several years, anyway. I throw a few coins in every year for her when I attend the medical."

I raised an eyebrow. "Medical?"

"In my, erm, position I have to have an annual medical before Christmas Eve. Like I said, the magic goes so far but it's still a big night. Have to make sure that I'm up to it. The world wants an old Santa with plenty of character, but at some point it becomes too much. Like for my dad."

"What happened to your dad?" I asked. I'd been curious ever since my arrival but it had seemed insensitive to ask.

Nick eyed me. "What happened to him? What do you mean?"

"Well, he's..." I stumbled for the right words.

"He handed over the baton and now he fills his time with hobbies. He's ice fishing right now."

"He's what? So you mean he isn't... dead?"

Nick's head spun towards me and he let out a laugh. "Oh, gosh, I guess I can see what you might have thought that. No, no, he's very much alive and well. You'll see him, I'm sure."

"He doesn't want to be around for all of this busy time?"

"I think he finds a trip to keep him away, actually. It forces me to manage without him instead of relying on him for everything. My parents both believe it's important for me to find my own way as Santa, not just copy what my father did. In fact, the only thing they've ever pressured me about is settling down and getting married."

"Your mum definitely wants to see that happen," I said.

"I get it. What I do is kind of crazy, and doing it all alone is a lot."

"Do you want to get married?" I asked.

"Of course. I believe I'll find the right woman and every-thing will fall into place. Just because it hasn't happened yet, I've not given up hope."

"Maybe you should put it on your Christmas list," I joked.

His eyes glistened as he looked at me. "Maybe I will."

We reached Claus Cottage and said hello to Cyril and Clive, who looked blue from the cold.

"Are you guys okay?" I asked.

Nick cocked his head to the side and smiled at me.

"We're fine, Miss. Get yourselves inside," one of the elf officers insisted. I couldn't remember which was which.

Nick opened the front door, still smiling.

"What's wrong with you?" I asked.

He laughed. "You, checking on the officers keeping my mother prisoner. I can see that Candy Cane Hollow is rubbing off on you."

21

Dinner was spiced carrot soup with fresh homemade bread, and the smell was divine.

The three of us sat at the table together and had just began to eat when the front door opened.

"Helloooooo!" A voice called out.

"In here, love," Mrs Claus responded.

I heard the trudge of boots and smiled at Ginger as she walked into the room.

"Well, this is a nice surprise," Mrs Claus said.

Ginger walked over and ruffled Nick's hair, exactly as an annoying sister would. He batted her hand away and she stuck out her tongue at him.

"Soup?" Gilbert offered.

"I won't say no," Ginger said, and took a seat. She yawned.

"Busy day, dear?"

"You know how it is. I'm not here to talk about me, though. How are you doing, stuck up here in this old place?"

Mrs Claus giggled. "Well, it's really been the most wonderful opportunity to catch up on some chores. I did snow art today with Holly, and I've started organising the photographs in chronological order."

"Sounds fun," Ginger deadpanned.

"I was thinking you could perhaps give me a bit of a lesson on sculpting, if the police will let me venture into the garden," Mrs Claus suggested.

"I can do that as long as you promise not to overtake my talent," Ginger agreed. Gilbert placed her soup in front of her and she reached across for a slice of bread and tore a hunk of it off. She dunked it into the bowl and ate greedily.

The doorbell rang and Gilbert gave an exaggerated huff as he stomped off to answer.

"He does hate when mealtimes are interrupted," Mrs Claus whispered.

"And I suppose you're here for a bowl of... oh, come in," we heard.

Nick turned in his chair to see who the visitor was.

Chief Superintendent Wiggles appeared and stood in the doorway. He didn't make eye contact with any of us.

"What is it, Walter? You don't need to be shy around us. And have a bowl of soup," Mrs Claus said.

Wiggles coughed and shook his head. "No, no thank you Mrs Claus. I'm afraid that I'm here to tell you we are charging you with the murder of Persephone Hyde-Barker. I've come to take you in to Candy Cane Custody. If you can gather a few belongings and come with me, please."

"Hold on, what is this?" Nick asked.

"She'll be held overnight and then presented at court in the morning to enter a plea," Wiggles said. The legal jargon sounded strange coming out of his mouth.

"You can't do this! Mrs Claus has stayed right here, like you asked. She's been feeding your police officers outside. She's obviously no murderer!" I exclaimed.

"She's been feeding who?" Wiggles raised an eyebrow.

"I've been feeding them!" Gilbert interjected.

"Yes, Gilbert has, that's what I meant," I said.

"And we all know that I wouldn't poison anyone, even if I do run a kitchen so dirty that Mrs Claus feels the need to..."

"Enough! Let's focus on the issue at hand. Wiggles, you can't possibly have enough evidence to charge my mum with murder," Nick rubbed his temple as he spoke.

"It's quite alright, dear. Walter's just doing his job and we won't make it any harder for him than it already is. I'll go and pack some things," Mrs Claus reached for Nick's arm and gave it a squeeze on her way out of the room.

"And I just wasted some of my soup on those elves out there! They could have given us a heads up. We could be halfway to Mistletoe Moor now. My cousin Graham would have helped us hide out."

"Gilbert!" Mrs Claus scolded him.

We all stood in a shellshocked silence as we listened to Mrs Claus climb the stairs to her bedroom.

"Wiggles, what's happened? Why the decision to charge her?" Nick asked when he was confident she was out of earshot.

"I told you, Nick, we have to get this case wrapped up before the big day. There are no other suspects. It was a Mrs Claus mince pie, that evidence is overwhelming. Even your mother admits that she made the murder weapon with her own hands!"

"But you know she isn't a murderer," Nick pleaded.

"That's not my job to decide. My job is to investigate and where there's the evidence, charge the right person. The court will decide whether she's guilty," Wiggles explained.

"As if that makes it better!" I exclaimed.

Mrs Claus' soft footsteps came down the stairs and she

returned to the room. She had filled a small holdall and changed into a warmer sweater.

"Now, Nick, when your father returns, tell him I love him. And of course I love you, my darling boy. Ginger, you have been like a daughter to me. And Gilbert, my cheeky helper, what fun you bring me every day. Not forgetting our newest addition to the family. Dear, sweet Holly. You have a home here, whenever you want it. Now, all of you be good and stay merry. It's the most wonderful time of the year, remember!"

"No," I said. My voice was firm and clear and everyone looked at me.

"No?" Wiggles asked.

"You can't do this. Mrs Claus isn't the murderer. I am. I killed Persephone," I heard myself say, as if in a dream.

"Holly, no!" Mrs Claus exclaimed.

"You did it?" Wiggles asked.

"No, she didn't. Don't do this, you wonderful girl," Mrs Claus said.

"I arrived in town on the day of the murder. You said yourself that that's suspicious, Wiggles. None of you have any idea of who I am. Maybe this wasn't my first murder. Maybe I just kill for the fun of it! No reason, no grudge against Persephone in particular..."

"Holly," Nick murmured, but I couldn't look at him.

"Lock me up," I said. I held my hands out and awaited the handcuffs.

To my horror, Wiggles began to laugh.

"What's so funny?" I asked. I'd never wanted to be a murder suspect before but all of a sudden I was offended not to be.

"You couldn't have done it. It's very admirable and all.

But Persephone ate the bite of that mince pie hours before you arrived in town," Wiggles said.

"Maybe I didn't arrive when you think I did! Maybe I came and, erm, left, and then came back!"

Wiggles rolled his eyes. "Mrs Claus, let's be going."

"It was me," Ginger said. She stood with her arms folded. Her eyes were full of tears.

"Ginger Rumples, you're confessing to murder?"

"I am. I was scared that Persephone was going to win the ice sculpture competition. I couldn't stand the thought of losing. I'm sorry that I ever got Mrs Claus messed up in this," she began to cry.

I stared at her, my mouth open. I'd just removed her from my own list of possible suspects and she was admitting it?

"Ginger, are you serious?" Nick asked.

"I'm sorry, Nick. I can't believe I've got your family involved in this after how good you've all been to me. I guess I didn't think it through."

"Ginger, dear, they're taking me. Let's just forget this conversation happened and everyone get a good night's sleep? Gilbert can make some hot cocoa. Everything will seem clearer in the morning," Mrs Claus said.

Wiggles shook his head beside her. "I don't know what's going on here anymore. Maybe the two of you both did it. Ginger Rumples, I'm charging you with the murder of Persephone Hyde-Barker. You'll need to accompany me to Candy Cane Custody now."

"Yes!" Ginger exclaimed and punched the air.

"Come on then, you two," Wiggles said.

"Us two?" Ginger asked.

"That's right. I've charged Mrs Claus and now I've

charged you too. We'll let the courts decide whether one of you did it or both of you," Wiggles said.

Ginger's shoulders slumped. "But it was me. I've admitted it and Mrs Claus has denied it. There's your answer."

"Oh, I wish it was that easy in my line of work. Come on, we need to get you two checked in before you miss supper."

Mrs Claus gave everyone a kiss goodbye, and then walked out with Chief Superintendent Wiggles. Ginger followed them at a snail's pace.

"Did you really do it?" Nick whispered to her.

"Of course not! But we can't let Mrs Claus take the blame for it. And Holly's effort was weak. She didn't even shed a pretend tear,' Ginger said with a frown.

"Hey! I tried!" I exclaimed.

"And I showed you how to do it properly. Now, the two of you need to sort this out. And quick!"

"We will," Nick and I said in unison.

22

Nick and I watched from the doorway as Mrs Claus, Ginger, Clive and Cyril were all somehow taken away in Wiggles' tiny Fiat. We remained there until the car's headlights had disappeared into the night, *Last Christmas* on repeat as they drove.

"I'm so sorry," I said, when Nick had closed the door and it was just the two of us in the hallway.

"Sorry? Why are you sorry?"

"I worry that I've been more of a distraction than a help to you. And now your mum and virtually your sister are both being charged with murder."

"Ginger's right. We have to work this out now. Come on, if we work together, we'll be able to figure this out."

We retired to the den and Gilbert soon appeared with hot cocoa, then excused himself for the night. We could hear him wailing through the house after he closed the door.

"He's really devoted to her," I said.

"Everyone is. Which is why it's so bizarre that someone

has killed in a way that frames her. I can't believe that anyone in Candy Cane Hollow would do that," Nick said.

"You're right. Although, there were those protesters at the sculpting competition."

"I'd forgotten about those," Nick admitted.

"Is there a way that we can find out who they were?" I asked.

"I could check CandyBook. Maybe there was an event arranged on there?"

"CandyBook?"

"It's like this social media site. You can, like, add friends and post photos. Some people arrange events on it."

Nick reached for his phone and I moved closer so that I could see his screen. Unsurprisingly, he had dozens of notifications and nearly as many friend requests.

"I don't really log on much," he explained.

He clicked across to the Events Nearby tab and scrolled through several – an ice fishing trip, a husky sled race, a reindeer care course.

"Milk and cookies! Here we are," he exclaimed.

"Mrs Claus Is A Killer Protest? That's subtle," I said.

"Five people attended. Or at least, said they were going to."

"Bring snacks!" I read.

"Everything's better with snacks," Nick shrugged.

"Those names mean anything to you?"

"Bill Taylor, Twinkle Hyde-Barker, Bonnie Butcher, Rascal Rumples and the event organiser himself Dane Hyde-Barker. Well, that's not a surprise. So, these are kids. Teenagers. They're all on the nice list, though."

"Well, that settles it then. Hold on, does it? Would the naughty list give you an idea of who the killer could be?" I asked.

Nick grimaced. "I don't know. Let's just say that record keeping isn't a strength of mine. My dad could have told you everything about everyone, but I'm not at that stage yet. I'm still kind of Santa in training, I guess. I wouldn't want to accuse someone of murder based on my poor filing skills."

"But these kids are on the nice list?"

"They're just exploring boundaries. Dane will be the leader, that's my guess. He does like to make his voice heard. It's like he's outraged about a different thing each day."

"Could he be a suspect?" I asked.

Nick shook his head. "I suspect the whole protest idea was just a teenage lark to them. It's fine, they can say what they want. They'll grow out of it. I mean, you might have guessed, Ginger wasn't the most compliant kid either."

"Yeah, that doesn't surprise me too much," I admitted. There was a certain spunk about her that I admired.

"I keep thinking about the computer," Nick said.

"Me too. I think it's still in the surgery."

"You do?"

"It didn't leave. At least not the day she was killed or the day after. I think it was hidden out of sight, and I don't know why."

"Well, I do have a skeleton key for all of the businesses in town," Nick said.

"You do?"

"A perk of the job," he said with a wink.

"And..."

"And let's go," he said.

We dived into fresh outdoor clothes, since our others were still soaked from the snowball fight, and Nick drove us to the High Street.

People and elves milled around, popping into shops and coffee lounges, but the surgery was closed and in darkness.

Nick pulled a huge set of keys from his pocket and spent some time trying to undo the door with the wrong lock. Eventually, we heard the click and the door opened.

Dozens of people must have seen us, but nobody seemed troubled by our breaking and entering. A perk of the job, as Nick had said.

The reception area was exactly as it had been the last time I'd been in there. The desk was clear.

Dr Lancaster's room was the opposite. He was clearly a man who desperately needed a secretary. His desk was overflowing with files, papers, old cups crusted over with congealed cocoa, and the remnants of at least four pizzas. The stench in the room was awful.

Before I could stop myself, I'd picked up an empty Styrofoam cup and tossed it into the waste-paper basket in the corner, where it landed on top of a syringe.

"This guy needs a wife," I heard myself mutter, then gasped and covered my mouth with my hands.

"Huh?" Nick said.

"I can't believe I just said that. What a sexist thing for me to say! I hope that's not why your mum is desperate for you to marry – so your wife can tidy up for you," I said.

Nick cocked his head and looked at me curiously. "I have no idea what you're talking about, but I can assure you I'm fully house trained. You may not have noticed that I placed both of our soaking wet clothes in the washing machine earlier after your vicious snowball attack."

My cheeks flamed as I remembered that he had done exactly that.

"That's very true. And I thank you for your service. Now, let's get looking. It can't be that easy to hide a computer, surely!"

We each tackled a separate area of the room, opening

cupboards and pulling out drawers. It was clear which parts of the room had been arranged and sorted by Persephone and which Dr Lancaster had had to use since her death. He seemed to have made a mess of every single thing he laid his hands on.

"You have to hope he's tidier when he's taking blood or something," I muttered.

A chill ran through me as the final piece fell into place.

"Nick," I exclaimed.

"What is it?" He asked, his head stuffed in a cupboard that was overflowing with junk.

"We're looking in here for the computer, because it never left. What if it's the same with the mince pie? Well, not the same, but opposite. What if we didn't see the mince pie arrive because it was already here."

"I don't follow," Nick scratched his head.

There was no time to explain, because the front door of the surgery opened.

23

I dashed across the room in an attempt to conceal both myself and Nick in the overflowing cupboard, but there wasn't enough time.

Behind us, the lights were flicked on and the sound of fingers drumming on the doorway made me shudder.

"Well, well. What a surprise. Nick? Are you well?" Dr Lancaster asked.

"All well, Doc, thanks. This is a random Claus Cleaning Check," Nick said.

"Really? I've never had one before," Dr Lancaster said with a smirk.

Nick cleared his throat. "Well, yes. This is awkward, Doc, but we've had reports about the place being a little, erm..."

"Disorganised!" I exclaimed.

"Disorganised, that's it..." Nick agreed.

"And we knew you must have so much to do until you can hire new help, so we decided to give you a hand," I said, then flashed him a grin.

"I find it hard to believe that Santa doesn't have more

important things to do than my paperwork," Dr Lancaster deadpanned.

"There's never anything more urgent than helping someone in need," Nick said.

Dr Lancaster surveyed the room with eyes wide, as if seeing the mess himself for the first time. "It really has got out of control."

"Yes," I agreed.

Dr Lancaster looked at me. I met his gaze. After a few moments, he broke the eye contact and stuffed his hands in his trouser pockets.

"I'll just use the little boy's room, then I'll come and help," he said.

I wondered whether to object, but decided not to.

He left the room and we heard him lock himself in the toilet just off the reception area.

"Did you know he'd hear about us being in here?" I asked Nick.

Nick smiled and that dimple flipped my stomach again. "Of course. Everyone in Candy Cane Hollow loves to be neighbourly."

"So, you agree?" I asked him.

He nodded, then gave a small gasp. I looked into the cupboard and saw what he'd found. Persephone's computer, the screen still adorned with stickers spelling out her name.

"Well, where do we start?" Dr Lancaster asked. I hadn't heard the toilet flush and his voice made me jump.

"Shall we set this back up?" I asked, as I gestured to the computer.

Dr Lancaster recoiled from it, his face ashen. "No, no, please. I look at it and see her. Just leave it there, please."

I glanced at Nick.

"You seem really upset about her death, Doc," he said.

"She was a fine secretary," Dr Lancaster said.

"You were in love with her," I said.

Dr Lancaster gazed up at the ceiling and allowed a smile to take over his face. "It's a cliché, isn't it? Falling in love with your secretary."

"That doesn't make it any less real," Nick said.

"Please, I'd rather speak to her," Dr Lancaster gestured towards me.

"No," Nick objected.

"It's fine. You can wait outside," I said with a courage I didn't feel.

"Are you sure?" Nick asked.

I nodded, and he brushed his hand against my own as he left the room.

"Is this better?" I asked.

Dr Lancaster nodded. "Take a seat."

I sat in the patients' chair and he sank down into the plush leather of his own seat. He relaxed immediately, his shoulders lowering and his posture at ease.

"I always wanted to be a doctor in a big city, a hospital full of hustle and bustle. Not here, not this," he waved his hand through the air as if the little messy room portrayed all of his failings.

"Why stay?" I asked, even as I suspected I knew the answer.

"For her, of course. I'd never met anyone like her before. At first, I thought I was being foolish to imagine that she'd share my interest. I'm not a great catch, I do know that. Not the most handsome and certainly not the most merry. But I did like to think I was a good man, at least."

"What happened?"

"She liked the status, I think. She would have been a

doctor's wife. The surgery would have become ours, a joint operation," he mused.

"I've heard that she was ambitious."

He laughed. "That's an understatement."

"How long were you together?"

"Oh, no, you misunderstand. We weren't together, not in any public sense anyway. It was more that we were two highly practical people considering the future. I laid my cards on the table and she asked for some time to think. I was a fool. I didn't want to pressure her. Even as I was waiting, I knew that it was hopeless. If I'd been such a catch, she wouldn't have needed weeks to think about it."

"You proposed, you mean?"

"I asked for her hand in marriage in return for her taking on half of the business," Dr Lancaster said.

I grimaced.

"Not the most romantic proposal, perhaps. But I knew that Percy had that competitive side. I wanted her to see the future we could build together."

"What happened?"

"She started spending more and more time with Mrs Claus. There was always a job that she was helping with, volunteering to do. I thought it was sweet at first, but then she started missing shifts here, turning up late. I'd ask her to ring a patient or check results and she'd tell me she was too busy working on something for Mrs Claus."

"That must have been infuriating," I said.

"I knew then that I'd lost her. Percy was always very focused on one thing. For a long time it was this surgery, and I stupidly allowed myself to believe that by extension it was me she was devoting her life to. When I had her focus, my goodness, it was as if the biggest spotlight had been turned on me. Such a wonderful feeling. To lose that..."

"It must have been horrible," I said.

"But you know all of this, don't you? You and Santa aren't really here to help me tidy up, are you?"

My cheeks flushed. "I had a suspicion."

"How?"

"You're the only person who called her Percy, for a start," I shared.

His eyes watered as he considered that. "She called me Si. Nobody in my life has ever shortened my name before. It's Sirus, my name. But normally I'm Dr Lancaster, or Doc at least. It felt so good to be given a nickname."

"And then, what? You were losing that connection because of Mrs Claus?" I asked.

Dr Lancaster frowned. "No, of course not. Mrs Claus was just a way in. Just as I was a way in to Percy almost owning a medical surgery. No, no... Percy had her eyes on a bigger prize."

I looked beyond Dr Lancaster and out through the window. Nick stood, watching us. I shivered as I understood.

"She wanted Nick," I murmured.

"She wanted Santa. She wanted to be the new Mrs Claus. And she knew that Mrs Claus was desperate for Nick to marry. All she had to do was be around, become familiar... but Nick barely knew who she was. It made Percy furious."

"And then the prize was announced for the sculpture competition," I said.

"Exactly. That required more time off. There was a big incident here one day, a patient had a seizure in reception while I was in with another patient. Percy should have been there, but she'd gone out to buy sculpting tools. That was when things reached a head," he looked down at his lap and shook his head.

"That's awful," I said.

"I was too harsh with her. I had to raise it, of course. But how was she to know that something like that would happen? She wasn't malicious, she was just very distracted. I told her that her attention needed to be back on her work. Even if she didn't want to accept my proposal."

I gasped. "She still hadn't given you an answer?"

"I'd waited almost three months. It sounds ridiculous saying it now, but she kept offering a glimmer of hope. I invited her to spend Christmas at my ski lodge over in Poinsettia Precinct, and she accepted. She bought me a fiancé card for my birthday. I'd just bought her a new car, and she was choosing carpets for the house we would buy. I think I'd started to imagine that she'd agreed without saying yes."

"She was really exploring all options, it sounds like," I said.

Dr Lancaster removed his glasses and wiped his eyes, rubbed his temple. "There's no fool like an old fool."

"So, you spoke to her?"

He nodded. "I spoke to her and it didn't go well. I think I pushed her into jumping. She made it very clear that she hadn't accepted my proposal and wouldn't be accepting it. She said some awful things about me, about us. She suggested the whole thing had been an illusion until she found something better, and told me that she had found something better."

"That's horrible," I said.

"I sent her home early that day. We needed space from each other. I hoped that things would blow over by the next day, that she'd race in and apologise and accept my proposal. Instead, she handed in her notice. She told me that she would have no time for work when she was married to Santa."

"She led you to believe that it was a done deal?" I asked.

"Oh yes, there was no doubt in her mind that she'd win him over and marry him. I was so angry. Humiliated! All of the years I'd wasted in this awful place because of her lies! I couldn't stand it. So I made us both a drink, and I served her a mince pie and I had a chocolate biscuit, and I suggested we call a truce."

"And the mince pie killed her," I said.

"Yes," he admitted.

"You killed her."

His eyelids drooped and his composure further sank into his chair. "I injected it straight into the mince pie. I know that Mrs Claus has been under suspicion, but I didn't plan it that way. I acted without a plan. For an hour, I thought it hadn't worked. I've never killed someone before, of course, and I guess I imagined it would have a more immediate reaction than it did."

"She didn't notice anything was wrong?" I asked.

"Oh, yes! She commented on the taste. She was very flustered about it, embarrassed for Mrs Claus in case a whole batch had gone out tasting that way. Even then, her loyalty was towards the Claus family!"

"She was obsessed with them like you were obsessed with her. Why did you move her computer?" I asked.

His cheeks flushed. "There were some, erm, accounting procedures that weren't entirely correct. I wanted to, erm..."

"Dr Lancaster?" I prompted.

He looked at me but his eyes were foggy, and then he slumped across his desk. The movement panicked Nick outside and I saw him dash out of sight, then a moment later heard him race in through the surgery door.

"Holly!"

"I'm okay. Call an ambulance. And the police," I said. I dove across to feel for a pulse, but there was none.

Wiggles arrived first, followed right away by the paramedics. They made their own attempts to search for a sign of life, then shook their heads.

"What happened?" Wiggles asked.

"I believe he gave himself a lethal dose of something when he went into the bathroom," I explained.

"And why would he do that?"

"He just confessed everything to me. Dr Lancaster killed Persephone Hyde-Barker, and he did it because he was jealous that he was losing her affections due to her infatuation with Nick Claus."

I looked up at Nick and saw his cheeks flush.

I wondered how high his modesty came on Persephone's list of things she liked about him.

It was near the top on mine.

24

Nick and I drove to collect Mrs Claus and Ginger from Candy Cane Custody, despite the late hour. We didn't want them staying away from home a moment more than they had to.

Mrs Claus emerged with curlers in her hair and Ginger carried an ice pick. She assured me she had been sculpting, not attempting an escape.

"They let you take an ice pick in there with you?" I asked in disbelief.

"Sure, why wouldn't they?" Ginger shrugged.

"I want to thank all of you for the efforts you went to for me. This has been quite the Christmas adventure!" Mrs Claus exclaimed.

"I'm just glad I get to see you guys released before I head home," I said with a smile.

"Oh Holly dear, we'll miss you so much. Are you sure you can't stay for Christmas Day?" Mrs Claus asked.

"I'd hate to impose," I said.

"Stay. Please," Nick said, his voice cracking as he spoke.

He reached for my hand and I allowed him to take it and give it a squeeze.

"Well, I guess I could. If you're sure you…"

"That's settled then," Ginger said, with a wink.

"Hey, it's officially Christmas Eve," Nick said. It was after midnight.

"The busiest day of the year for you?" I asked.

"He needs a good woman by his side, dear. It's too much responsibility for one person," Mrs Claus said.

"Mother!" Nick exclaimed as he parked the car outside Claus Cottage. It looked strange to see the place without Cyril and Clive shuddering away in the cold.

"It's a mother's job to interfere, Nicholas. Ah, look, your father's home!"

We all climbed out of the car and as we walked up the path, the door opened. Standing there in a red velour tracksuit with a white beard down to his belly button, was the Santa of my childhood. The Santa of my imagination.

I stood open mouthed.

"Well, ho ho ho! Welcome to Claus Cottage, Holly. Merry Christmas!"

To my horror, I burst into tears. Father Christmas came out and wrapped his arms around me, and he smelled of nutmeg and cloves and a little bit of fish too. I closed my eyes and allowed myself to give in to the wonder of Christmas.

"Hello, Santa," I whispered as he held me.

"Dad! Come on, you guys will freeze" Nick called.

"Jealous that he's hugging your girl?" Ginger teased.

We piled indoors and collapsed into our beds. By the time I woke up, Nick and his dad had already left. It really would be the busiest day of Nick's year, but it wasn't much less frantic at Claus Cottage.

We played Christmas songs endlessly and all of us – Mrs Claus, Gilbert, Ginger and I – baked rack after rack of cookies and mince pies, then we set out and delivered them by hand to as many people as we could.

By the time we returned home, it was Christmas Day evening, and we curled up in the den together by the roaring fire and watched Christmas movies. Ginger disappeared at one point and then returned with old photograph albums. She delighted in pointing out a young Nick in the middle of eating a worm, and another one of him wearing one of her old tutus.

"If you're going to marry into this family, Holly, you need to know what you're getting," she said.

"Marrying? Did you say marrying?" Mrs Claus perked up.

"Nobody's marrying anyone! I'm staying for tomorrow and then I really do have to think about going home. I have to find a new job, remember," I said.

"Well, we are in need of a new doctor right here," Mrs Claus said.

I rolled my eyes and returned my attention to the TV. These festive films were great escapism, with their happy endings, but that wasn't real life. Not my real life, at least.

As we all said goodnight, I excused myself to ring August, and as I stood on the doorstep, I could almost have believed that I saw Santa and a sleigh pulled by reindeers flying overhead.

I shook my head, unsure what was real anymore.

August didn't answer the phone. No doubt she was deeply involved in some intricate Christmas Eve tradition for baby Jeb, and good for her.

"I'm just calling to wish you all a wonderful Christmas. I

love you and I can't wait to see you soon," I left my message after the beep.

The next morning, I was the last to wake up.

I padded downstairs and heard the noise of excited people attempting to be quiet. Everyone was in the den and I gave them each a hug. Seeing Nick's father was still hard to believe.

"Let's open gifts!" Mrs Claus sounded as excited as a small child.

"Gifts! Oh no, I didn't get anyone anything," I apologised.

"Holly, dear, we're the Claus family. We give the gifts," Mrs Claus said with a wink.

Everyone had a small, but beautiful gift.

Ginger opened a new ice pick engraved with her initials and joked that she'd use it on the turkey over lunch.

Gilbert had a blow torch and promised to use it to craft the perfect crème brulee ready for dessert.

Nick's dad had a pair of slippers that were actually huge Brussels sprouts. He roared with laughter and put them on straight away.

Mrs Claus opened a scarf embroidered with the Claus family crest, and was so touched by it that she cried.

Nick was last to open, and he grinned as he saw what looked like an ornate pocket watch. "Dad?"

"It's your turn, son," Father Christmas said.

I leaned in to get a better look.

"This is the Christmas Eve timepiece. It controls every-thing. Each Santa hands it down to the next when they've finished their training."

"It's beautiful," I said.

Ginger cleared her throat. "Are we missing a box or what?"

My cheeks flushed. "Oh, my goodness, no. I'm a guest! Being here with you all is more than enough, really."

"I do have something for you. Can we take a walk?" Nick asked.

I bit my lip and nodded, then allowed him to pull me up from the carpet. We pulled on our outdoor clothes and I trudged through Claus Cottage after him.

"I really can't thank your family enough for this, Nick," I said as we walked across the lawn.

"We've loved having you. Everyone loves you, Holly."

He stopped walking once we were out of sight of the cottage and I looked up at him. He took a breath.

"Your Christmas wish," he said.

"Oh, that was just..." I said as my cheeks flushed. Why had I made such a silly wish instead of asking for a perfume or a new apron or something? I thought back to my wish and cringed.

All I want for Christmas is... to belong.

"I think we can make it come true here. I think you've already made it come true here. I know you have a life in London, I'm just asking you to consider staying here. We'd love to have you," Nick said.

"You all would?" I asked with a smile.

"Me especially. And I don't know what you're doing on New Year's Eve, but I don't have a date to the Ball."

"Is that an invitation, Nick Claus?"

"I believe it might be, Holly Wood."

"Okay, enough with my full name! I'd love to be your date," I said.

"Really? Yes!"

"Hey, Nick, do you make your own Christmas list?" I asked.

He leaned in and whispered to me, "All I want for Christmas is you."

THE END

Get your copy of the next book, Slay Bells Ring, now at mybook.to/christmas2